"When did you learn to steal? Son, how could you have turned from my wonderful small boy into a...a sneak thief?"

Richard's head moved. Just a very tiny bit to the left, toward Dad. "I'm not your son," he said. His shirt, his face, and now his eyes, were shiny wet. "Don't you remember?"

Carolyn Desmond, Richard's twelve-year-old half-sister, tells the story of the summer that devastated her family. It is Carolyn who is first suspicious of Flim-flam, Richard's conniving pal, now hanging around more than ever. And it is Carolyn who worries when, in the course of the summer, Richard decides to try to contact his father; though he has been raised with love and discipline by his stepfather, Richard has never let himself forget about his own father, who abandoned him when he was two years old. As pressures build and the truth becomes clear, the Desmonds find themselves facing the kind of crisis that tests both their strength and their compassion.

Once again, as in her popular *Welcome Home, Jellybean*, Marlene Fanta Shyer captures the verve, the language, the outlook of the young people about whom and for whom she writes.

My Brother, the Thief

MARLENE FANTA SHYER

Charles Scribner's Sons
New York

Special thanks to
Judge Matthew Coppola of Family Court
Police Commissioner William Hegarty
Det. William Flowers, Youth Officer
Lt. Joseph Guarasci, Community Affairs Officer
of the City of New Rochelle, N.Y.
and to
Barton Reissig, Supervising Probation Officer
of the City of White Plains, N.Y.
for the information that inspired the theme of my book
and made a fictional young thief less so.

M.F.S.

Library of Congress Cataloging in Publication Data

Shyer, Marlene Fanta.
My brother the thief.

SUMMARY: Twelve-year-old Carolyn tries to deal with the knowledge that her 16-year-old brother Richard and his shady friend Flim-flam are thieves.
[1. Stealing—Fiction] I. Title.
PZ7.S562My [Fic] 80-343
ISBN 0-684-16434-5

1 3 5 7 9 11 13 15 17 19 F/C 20 18 16 14 12 10 8 6 4 2

Printed in the United States of America

For Judi Ross
to whom, surprisingly, no one has ever dedicated a book before

ONE

My brother, Richard, had two secrets. One was that although he was almost sixteen, he had never learned to swim. The other was much, much worse.

When I discovered his second secret, I was afraid he was absolutely going to cream me. It wouldn't have been hard, either. I am almost four years younger and lots shorter. Richard says the only place I've got muscles is in my mouth.

I must have them in my eyes, too, because when I was home sick that day last spring, I saw what I saw in his room as clear as anything. A bug had landed in my throat, and before my mother left for work, she looked in there and said, "Very red, Carolyn," took my temperature, and told me to stay home from school.

My pleasure. I love watching morning game shows on television, reading old books, working on a scrapbook of my life, just doing nothing. I also love snooping around. When I finished snooping around in my parents' room (my mother is tidy and there is not much to see if you don't open drawers, which I'm not allowed to do), snooping around the refrigerator (two yogurts, a hunk of cheese, and fruit, fruit, fruit because my father is diet-crazy), I headed for Richard's room. He has signs on his door: "Off Limits," "No Trespassing," "Stay Out," and "Do Not Enter." I went in.

Well, why not? You don't think he'd stay out of *my* room, do you? I'd have to hire a guard with a gun to sit at the door if I wanted to keep him out once he catches the scent of candy bars, a new record, or sharpened pencils. Besides, he was away at school, I wouldn't touch a thing, and who'd know?

Right away I saw it—something purple, shiny, and strange under his bed.

For a long time I stood in the doorway trying to figure out what could be purple and practically glowing fluorescent that Richard would have under his bed. The only other thing I ever saw under there was the old suitcase he bought at Mrs. Covelli's garage sale for fifty cents, and a few dirty magazines.

Purple and shiny, shiny and purple. I moved closer. Richard's signs really had me spooked; I felt as if any minute an arm would come out of the ceiling and punch me in the nose for trespassing. Still, I went in.

I knelt next to the bed and peered under the springs, careful not to disturb the broken-down kite hanging over Richard's bed. Very carefully, in case it was a purple cobra or a man-eating eggplant, I reached under the bed and pulled it out.

Oh, big deal. A swim team jacket. Brand new, very shiny, with white letters on the back: NEW MADISON SHORE CLUB SWIM TEAM. Someone must have left it at our house, or maybe Richard was holding it for one of the team members. Even though Richard can't swim, we belong to the New Madison Shore Club, so it was no surprise that Richard had the jacket. But why under the bed? And wow, now I spotted another one back there, way in the corner. *Two* team jackets?

I couldn't ask, of course, or he'd figure out that I'd been in his room, so I carefully bunched it up the way I'd found it and shoved it back under there. I took a few minutes to look over some other junk he had lying around—old keys, a skull bank that glows in the dark, an x-ray of a person's foot he found in a garbage can a couple of months ago, a half-eaten roll of Lifesavers. I was dying for a grape one, the one next in line, but didn't dare. I just went back to my own room and swallowed my twelve o'clock aspirin and then went down to the kitchen to make myself a sandwich.

My mother called a little after noon from her job as a teller in the New Madison Savings and Loan. "Carolyn, are you all right? How are you feeling, dear?" she asked.

"I'm okay," I said. I didn't want her to worry about me, but I didn't want her to send me back to school either.

"Did you take your aspirin?" she asked, and then followed up with her lunchtime series of other questions: What had I eaten? Was I lying down? Was there enough orange juice? And what was I doing?

"Not much," I said, and my mind zipped back to the purple jackets under Richard's bed.

Then she wanted to know if I had a headache.

"No," I said, but by the time I hung up, one was starting.

Richard is really only my half-brother. About two years after he was born, his real father disappeared. One day he packed his bags and left and never came back. Once or twice he sent Richard birthday cards, one Christmas he sent a five-dollar bill, and on Richard's seventh birthday he sent the big plastic red-white-and-blue kite that Richard has had hanging over his bed for over eight years. Actually the kite was in a kit, and my own father helped Richard put it together. My father said the directions with it weren't very clear, so it never could fly well, and I suppose that's why Richard just hung it over his bed and forgot about it.

But he never forgets about his father. Just recently I heard him asking my mother where in New Mexico she thought his last birthday card had been sent from.

My mother never likes to talk about Richard's father. Whenever Richard brings up the subject, I've noticed she gets very busy, either cleaning out cupboards or throwing wash into the machine, or raking leaves or something, as if she doesn't want to give the subject her full attention and thinks that if she leaves out information here and there, it will look as if she's too busy with whatever else she's doing. Last time, though, she did say that Richard's father used to supply food in trucks to factory workers and he worked very hard until the factories began putting vending machines into their cafeterias and put Richard's father right out of business. That's when he left. Then Richard wanted to know where his father's parents were, his grandparents.

"Dead, I'm afraid," my mother said, and that closed the subject.

My own father married my mother a year after Richard's father left. After I was born, my father adopted Richard and changed his name from Searles to Desmond, our family name. Richard doesn't really remember his father at all and calls my father Dad, and once I heard my father tell Richard that if he could have had his own son, if he had sent up an order to the Manufacturer of Kids, he would have ordered a boy just like Richard.

When my father came home the night I had the bug, he sat with me in the den and took his turn reading the thermometer that came out of my mouth.

"You're fine, Carolyn," he said, "and you can go back to school tomorrow. That's the bad news. The good news is you don't have to set the table tonight or scrape the plates."

My father has this crazy idea that if we don't do chores, we will either fall apart into lazy pieces or grow up to be rotten people lying around in gutters, so if he can't think of something that needs doing, he makes something up, believe it or not. That's one of his big faults. He worked his way through high school and college and dental school and thinks everybody should work his or her way through something. He thinks working hard will make people perfect. He also thinks eating right will make people perfect—which comes from being a dentist, I guess. He says junk food will make our teeth fall out of our heads, and if he had his way he'd have a skull and crossbones put on every package of cookies and cake in the supermarket. The skull would have no teeth.

Since Dad loves to see kids work until they drop, Richard and I water the plants, take out the garbage, polish the tennis trophies Dad won before he got knee trouble, run to the store—you name it. Dad said that when he was a kid, he used to have to beat the rugs, which was a terribly strenuous job, and weren't we lucky that now we had vacuum cleaners and electric brooms? Richard said Dad must have inhaled too much dust and it made him creaky.

"Creaky" is Richard's favorite word.

"Hey, where'd you get those creaky new shoes?" Richard asked when his friend came over after dinner in a pair of Western boots with fringes.

"In a foot locker, ha, ha."

The friend's name is John Sullivan, but everybody calls him Flim-flam. His father is dead and he lives with his mother and her boyfriend.

"Where'd you get the name Flim-flam?" I asked him again. I'd been asking him that since the day he first started coming to the house a couple of months ago, but he'd never tell me. This time he didn't even look at me. In fact, he seemed really anxious to get out of our kitchen, as if he was covering something up. His face had the same guilty look as the day I caught him with his hands on my bike lock and he said he was just going to try to guess the combination.

"M.Y.O.B.," Richard said, and Flim-flam just laughed and followed Richard upstairs. Richard taught me that "M.Y.O.B." stands for Mind Your Own Business when I was about two years old, and he never lets me forget it.

I saw Dad give Mom a look and I knew what it meant: They didn't care for Flim-flam but didn't want to make remarks in front of me. My parents are always protecting me from hearing anything really interesting—their conversations in front of me are strictly G-rated—because anything interesting is "not meant for twelve-year-old ears."

They don't understand that although my ears are only twelve years old, the rest of me sometimes feels like a hundred. Like a few minutes later, when Richard and Flim-flam left, everything looked great and seemed fine. Richard kissed my mother good-by and said they were going to Flim's to study, and Flim said, "Have a nice evening, folks," and my mother said, "Aren't you going to take a sweater? It's chilly tonight," and Richard said, "I'll be okay," and they left—but not before I'd caught sight of something turned inside out and bunched up under Flim-flam's arm as they were heading out the back door.

I pretended to be going to the kitchen for a glass of water, but I really wanted to look out the window to the back of the driveway where Flim-flam had his car, and then I saw what I wish I hadn't seen. Now I knew what Flim-flam had been covering up. My brother and Flim-flam were putting on the purple, shiny jackets, which were practically glowing in the dim light coming from the garage.

I started to think fast. Anyone could buy the team jackets, of course, but only the team members wear them, and the kids at the club all knew who was on the team and who wasn't. Maybe Richard wanted to impress the rest of the world. He might even be going as far as East Loomis, where he'd be sure not to run into any real members of the team.

One thing was sure. The jackets didn't belong to anyone we knew—no one had left them in our house.

Maybe my brother or Flim-flam had stolen them!

TWO

For a long time I told myself I was wrong. It's very hard to think your own brother may be a thief, especially when he is really a good kid most of the time. I remember once when I was little and fell off my bike and scratched my legs and was lying on the sidewalk screaming my head off because I thought I would bleed to death right there next to the fire hydrant, Richard ran around ringing doorbells until he got our neighbor, Mrs. Covelli, to drive me to the emergency room at the hospital. He even gave up playing kickball to come to sit in the back of her car with me, and although he kept saying, "Shut up, you're all right," it made me feel much better having him there.

So I put the purple jackets out of my mind until the last week of June. School was over and my father got the idea that Richard should paint the inside of our beach locker. I got the job of painting the door and sweeping the floor. As soon as Dad thought up these assignments, he got into a wonderful mood and began talking about what a marvelous summer we were all going to have at the club this year. Then he looked at

Richard out of the corner of his eye and said, "We have a new swim coach this year. Shall we sign you up for swimming lessons?"

He has been asking Richard the same question every year since I can remember, and Richard always says no. This year Richard said, "Definitely no."

My father, still in a warm mood, said, "Why not, Rich?" and Richard said, "Not interested."

Of course, I know Richard is very interested. The problem is that if my father signed Richard up for swimming lessons, even private ones, within ten minutes everyone at the club would know that Richard can't even float. For years, ever since he had a small infection in his right ear, he's been telling everyone that it's his ear trouble that's been keeping him out of the pool. Richard has always been scared to death of the water because of something that happened when he was very little. It's something my mother knows and won't tell me, probably because it "isn't meant for twelve-year-old ears."

Nothing is meant for twelve-year-old ears, and plenty is meant for twelve-year-old hands: garbage pails, the garden hose, paintbrushes. Dad drove Richard and me to the beach by way of the hardware store, where we each got paint, a brush, a wooden stirrer, a cardboard bucket, and a free paper hat to paint in. We fought a bit about which station on the car radio we were going to listen to and who got to sit in front with Dad (this time Richard won, the fink), and then Dad supervised while I swept the locker floor and spread the newspapers. Finally Dad said he was off to work and left us with six hundred instructions and said he'd pick us up at five o'clock.

Richard was not in a painting spirit. He said he had lots better things to do than paint lockers. He said yellow was a creaky color, and why wouldn't Dad go along with his idea of bright orange with green trim? And he said I looked like a Chinese Communist in his old shirt and my paper hat and to take the hat off before anyone who might know us saw me.

Then music came blaring out of the locker next to ours and it happened to be coming out of a portable radio that was playing Richard's (not my) station. Our lockers are like connecting wooden rooms built in long rows, sort of like friendly prison cells with doors instead of bars. There's room for a bench and some shelves and my rubber raft, and there are hooks for bathing suits on the walls. The walls are just nailed-together planks, and sounds travel, including music. Pretty soon, the owner of the radio appeared.

"Hello. My name is Phillipa Ravelle, but everyone calls me Cookie," she said.

Richard did a double-take, not because she had a funny voice that sort of went up and down, but because she was really pretty. She had light-brown hair, very long and very straight except for a few dips and swirls around her face, and a sort of happy, smiling mouth. She was wearing little silver star earrings and a yellow bathing suit. "Look at that! I match your locker!" she said, and she came over and stood next to the place Richard had painted yellow over the old light-green paint to show us. "What a pretty color!" she said, and Richard said, "It's not bad."

Then *I* did a double-take because he'd just finished telling me the awful things the color reminded him of.

"Want some potato chips?" Cookie offered. Her voice went down on "want some" and up on "potato chips." I took some and Richard said, "Thanks, maybe later."

"Are you new at the club?" Richard asked her then. She said she was and said she intended to try out for the diving team, and then Richard got very quiet and busy with his brush.

"Do you dive?" she asked.

"No."

"Do you sail?" Cookie asked and Richard said, "No. Ever since I had an ear infection I haven't been big on water sports."

Cookie bit into a chip and said, "Oh, that's too bad. I love water sports," and there was a big silence. "In fact, my father just bought a sunfish."

"Wow!" I said. I've always wanted to go out on one of those little boats.

"You want to go for a sail?" Cookie asked, and I said "Yes" loud and clear, although I think she wanted Richard to go. He just kept painting like crazy, as though the wall were going to sink into the floor if he didn't get the brush moving up and down a mile a minute. He didn't say a thing.

Cookie and I went for a short sail, and she told me she'd moved to New Madison last year from Duluth, loved anything silver, and was allergic to penicillin, wheat germ, chocolate, almonds, ragweed, and Abyssinian cats. I told her Richard was allergic to feather pillows, and she said, "I am too!" and got very interested. She asked me a whole bunch of questions about Richard—what sort of music he liked, what sign of the horoscope he was born under (Libra), what his other allergies were. "I don't know, you'll have to ask him yourself," I said, and she said she would.

And did. The minute we got back to the locker, and with the radio for background music, she started asking Richard this and that. Pretty soon, while I was busy painting the locker door, she and Richard were sitting on the floor sharing a Pepsi and blabbing their heads off.

Until Flim-flam arrived. For once, I guessed that my brother was not too thrilled to see his friend. "Hey, Mother, what are you doing?" Flim asked. Flim-flam calls Richard

"Mother" only when no grownups are around. Especially real mothers.

"How'd you get in here?" Richard wanted to know. Flim-flam is not a member of the New Madison Shore Club but seems to be around more than the regular members.

"I told the man at the gate my mother had the car with the club sticker on it, and he let me right in," Flim-flam said, grinning his head off, mainly in the direction of Cookie. "Gonna introduce me to your new friend?"

Right off I could see my brother was not in any hurry to introduce Flim to Cookie, but he is always polite when girls are around, so he made a quick introduction.

Flim-flam picked up a brush and said he'd help paint the locker, but after giving the wall a couple of streaks he said Richard and I were crazy for using old-fashioned brushes when a roller could do the job in about five minutes, and look how long it was taking me to just paint the door.

That's when I made the mistake of saying that it wasn't taking me a bit long, that if I hadn't been out on Cookie's boat I would have finished the door long ago.

Flim-flam's ears went right up. "Cookie has a boat?" he asked, and now it was *his* voice that was going up and down—mostly up.

Cookie nodded.

"So how about a sail?" Flim-flam asked, still grinning his head off.

"Okay," Cookie said. I couldn't tell if she really wanted to take him or not, but I could tell that Richard sure as anything was down on the whole idea. Cookie turned to Richard as she and Flim-flam started to leave. "Sure you don't want to come, too? There's room for one more on the boat."

"Gotta get with it and paint this locker," Richard said, and he leaped up and started practically throwing the paint on the walls.

As soon as they'd left, he turned to me with murder in his eyes. "You are some creaky kid," he said. "When are you going to learn that silence is golden?"

"Okay, Mother," I said.

That night after dinner, when I'd finished scraping and rinsing and taking out the garbage (Dad said we were lucky to have garbage to take out, believe it or not), I decided to go up to my room and write a letter to my best friend, Jen, who had just left for the summer to visit her grandmother in Utah. Someone had "borrowed" my pencils and ballpoints, and that someone was sitting in his own room with the stereo headphones clamped to his ears like he was getting interplanetary messages from Jupiter or Saturn. Without meaning to, my eyes went right to the spot under his bed where I'd seen the purple jackets and—oh, no!—there was something lying there I'd never seen before, something new and black and shiny—and I knew that whatever it was, Richard couldn't have bought it. He had just told Dad this afternoon on the way home from the club that he was down to two dollars in his bank account and hinted that he could use a little payment for painting the locker. Dad had been pretty pleased with the job we did but suggested that we buy deck paint and really do a job by painting the floor. He said we'd talk about payment later. So at the moment, Richard was broke.

Which is why I knew immediately that whatever that black and shiny thing was, it could not have been *bought* by Richard.

"What's that under your bed, Richard?" I asked. I hoped Richard would notice the way my eyebrows, eyes, and mouth all looked suspicious, the way television detectives look when they know for sure who tried to throw the leading lady off the bridge.

Richard, of course, could not hear me.

"What's that under your bed?" I screamed at him about three times. Finally he took one earphone off and let the question sink in.

"Dust," he said.

"No, on top of the dust!" I screamed, pointing.

I narrowed my eyes, tilted my head to one side, and asked Richard where the heck he'd gotten a beautiful pair of new fins if he was broke at five o'clock when Dad picked us up.

"Dad put them under my bed to surprise me," Richard said. "For painting the locker. There was a five-dollar bill stuck in one of them, too."

Wow! Had I ever been wrong! Then I thought if Richard got a gift for painting the locker, maybe I got one for painting the door! Sure enough, when I flew back in my own room and looked under my own bed, I found a pair of the swim goggles I'd wanted so badly since last summer and a couple of singles tied to them with a rubber band.

I had to go back and apologize to Richard for being so suspicious—and I had the funny feeling that if I'd been wrong about the fins, I could have been wrong about the jackets. Maybe Flim-flam borrowed them or found them, or something. "Sorry, Rich," I said, but he had put the earphones back on his head and didn't hear me.

But then I remembered what I'd originally come for and went to Richard's desk to find a pen or pencil—and saw something else I'd never seen before: a little silver pen-flashlight not bigger than one of my pencils lying next to it. Not that I can keep track of everything Richard owns—but because I'm always in there trying to find one of my own ballpoints, I do know a new desk thing when I see it. I was about to ask him where that had come from when Dad called me to the telephone. Jen was calling me all the way from Utah because she really missed me and her grandmother had allowed her to call me if we only talked for three minutes. She said she was going to send me a picture postcard to paste in my life scrapbook.

"I miss you, too, Jen," I told her. She sounded just as close as if she were calling from her house around the corner.

"Who are you hanging around with?" she asked me, knowing that Barbara, our other friend, was already getting ready to pack her trunk for camp.

"Just Richard," I said.

Jen sighed. "I feel sorry for you, I really do," she said. Then she threw in a couple of "yuks" to show me what she thought of my brother.

"Well, he's not all that bad," I said, and our three minutes were up.

When I got back to Richard's room I noticed the penlight wasn't on his desk. "What happened to that skinny flashlight that was here a minute ago?" I asked him.

"What flashlight?" he said.

"The silver one. And where'd you get it, anyhow?"

"You must have imagined it," Richard said. "Can't you see I'm busy?"

"Busy doing what?" I challenged.

"Busy waiting for you to disappear out of my room," he said.

THREE

About a week later my father thought up a brand-new chore. He was going to Philadelphia for the day to give a lecture at a college and wouldn't be needing his car, so Richard was assigned to wash the outside and I was to vacuum the inside, including the trunk. Also, Richard had to sweep out the garage, and I had to bike over to the supermarket and buy my father cottage cheese, carrots, and a pineapple. He and my mother were starting a new diet. My mother took me aside and told me I could buy myself a pint of Heavenly Hash ice cream but not to talk about it. She knows I'm crazy about Heavenly Hash and says a scoop now and then isn't going to hurt me. (I think she takes a scoop now and then herself, when Dad's asleep.)

Richard loves Dad's car. It isn't very new and isn't a Rolls Royce or anything, but it has a shiny bronze finish and bucket seats. By October Richard figures he's going to have his license and Dad will let him use the car weekends, so he doesn't mind washing and waxing it, to sort of keep it in good shape. He actually puts his heart into sudsing up the soap and circling all over the roof with a big sponge and wiping the windows until they look as if they're not there.

Right after I'd done my job, cleaned up every crumb and piece of lint in sight, I told Richard I was going to the store and left the driveway, glad to have it over with. I went into the kitchen, where I found the five-dollar bill Mom had left me under the salt shaker. Suddenly I heard a car drive up, and a few seconds later Flim-flam's voice coming through the open window. He seemed to be arguing with Richard, and what got me really interested was that they were obviously trying to keep the argument very quiet, as if they were fighting in a library. Richard kept saying, "Shh. Do you want the whole creaky neighborhood to hear?"

I heard Flim-flam say, "Calm down, Mother. You are some nervous cat," and then I heard, "Keep cool, I'll just show it to you," and I got *very* interested. Whatever he was going to show Richard was something I didn't want to miss, so I flew to the window and hoped that they wouldn't notice me through the screen.

They didn't. On the other hand, whatever it was that Flim-flam had brought over to show Richard was under a white sheet in his trunk, wrapped up very tight and about the size of a mini-mummy.

Then I heard Richard say that he wanted no part of hiding whatever it was and I saw him shake his head about seventeen times. I also saw him wave his arms trying to get rid of the cloud of smoke from a little cigarette Flim was smoking—obviously pot, from the smell that was drifting into the kitchen.

Flim-flam said, "Did it hurt to keep the jackets under your bed for one night? Did it? Can I help it if my old lady and her old man practically search me every time I walk into the house?"

Then Richard said, "Listen, that reminds me, I don't want

the jacket. Thanks, but no thanks. I'm giving it right back to you. I don't know why I even put it on that night. I guess I just wanted to see how it looked."

"Keep it, it looks good on you."

"I don't want it!"

Flim-flam said, "Okay, okay. Square business," which is Flim-flam talk for "Don't worry. Everything's okay."

"And I don't want the flashlight. I don't even want to know where you got it. I don't need it. I don't have to see in the dark."

Good for you, Richard, I thought.

"Oh, come on, keep it. It's not the Hope Diamond, Mother!"

Richard shrugged. "Okay, okay, I'll keep it," he said.

Not okay, Richard, I thought.

I watched Flim-flam take the last drag from his joint, then throw it on the ground and grind out the butt. Richard quickly kicked driveway gravel over it.

"Okay, Rich, stay cool. How about you just stick this piece of merchandise in your room until tomorrow?"

Richard said, "Keep it in your trunk. They won't look there."

"Listen, Mother, this is my old lady's car. All she has to do is open the trunk and I'm dead."

"I'm not doing it, Flim-flam. Forget it."

"Okay, buddy. . . . Some friend. Some hero. But don't expect me to do any favors for you either. Don't expect me to keep your secrets—like there's nothing wrong with your ears except they're gonna sink right to the bottom of the pool with the rest of you. That would be asking altogether too much, Mother."

Richard's face turned the color of the soapsuds on the fenders. He said something that I couldn't hear, a bunch of words he seemed to swallow right down into his neck. Then I heard Flim-flam say, "Like what would Cookie think? Wouldn't she have a big laugh?" Pretty soon Flim-flam and Richard just lifted the white-sheeted thing out of Flim-flam's trunk and began carrying it into our house through the garage.

I grabbed the chance to fly out the front door so they wouldn't know I'd been there—but not before I heard Flim-flam laugh and say, "Square business, Mother. You're one of us."

When I got back from the store with the groceries, the car was sparkling in the sun in the driveway, the garage door was closed, and Richard and Flim-flam were gone. As soon as I put the groceries away, I raced up to my brother's room to check out what was under the bed.

With my heart pounding like a disco beat and my knees wobbling like I'd just learned to walk, I stood in the doorway staring at the white-sheeted lump that was pushed way back against the wall where nobody was supposed to see it.

I could never win a pennant for valor. I am scared of things nobody else is scared of, like harmless spiders, the assistant principal— and mystery packages, stolen from who-knows-where and wrapped in white sheets. Could be anything, couldn't it? An ancient Egyptian mummy taken from the museum at midnight, ready to put the evil eye on me for touching it?

Silly. It was clearly nothing that would bite, scratch, or squirt me with deadly poison. I leaned over, put out my hand, and stretched out my fingers to touch the sheet, to get an idea if the thing under it was soft or hard. Hard. Hard as a gravestone.

But when I finally pulled off the sheet, I saw only a harmless bass guitar, the kind they have in the window of Jack's Music Store on Main Street. The kind that costs so much money it would take a hundred years to save up for it.

I really shivered then. This was worse than a mummy. What if Richard got caught with this thing under his bed? I pictured a policeman pulling handcuffs out of his pocket and snapping them around my brother's wrists—with a stolen something this valuable in his room, the idea was not far-fetched. Shaking, I wrapped it up tight again and shoved it back where I'd found it.

Then I ran downstairs and went straight to the freezer. Heavenly Hash ice cream always makes me feel better. I ate a scoop, and that gave me time to think. Then I ate another scoop. This batch seemed better than any I'd ever had. I had one more scoop, every bit delicious.

I thought of telling my mother. Impossible. Like me, she gets headaches, only mine are in the front of my head and hers are in the back, and much worse. Tell my father? Forget that. He doesn't get mad often, but when he does, it's like the hurricanes we sometimes have in September when we have to take in all the porch furniture. Dad's temper could bend trees and make folding chairs fly.

I could tell Richard I knew, threaten him like Flim-flam did if he didn't get rid of the guitar. It wasn't a bad thought. The problem is that Richard knew *my* secret. And he wouldn't stop at telling my friends; he'd tell the world.

My secret is really, really embarrassing. My name is Carolyn F. Desmond, and the "F" stands for Frankfurter. Believe it or not. What was my mother thinking of to name me Carolyn Frankfurter? She was thinking of my grandfather. It was his name. I don't care if it is a family name and that it means that someone back in our history came from Frankfurt, and that there was a distinguished judge once with the same name. My mother must have beaten some rugs in her day, too, and gotten some dust in *her* head to have given me a middle name that could ruin my life if word got out.

I remember when it leaked out that Heather Engstrom's mother liked gardens so much she'd given all her kids two flower names. When the kids found out Heather's middle name was Lilac, they sprayed everything in her desk with perfume and painted her gym sneakers purple. For a week Heather smelled as if she'd slept at the florist's. I imagined the kids filling my desk with sauerkraut and painting my sneakers with mustard. Richard may have his problems, but at least he has a nice, simple middle name—David, his father's name. Life is not fair.

I got the ice-cream bowl and spoon washed up just in time. I was sticking the Heavenly Hash into the back of the freezer when Mom came home. Of course, I'd left a spot of ice cream on the kitchen table, and she saw it right away. Giving me a wink, she headed right for the refrigerator and said, "Forget pineapple and cottage cheese" and "Don't tell your father." She took the same bowl I'd used and helped herself to a scoop, and I sat with her while she told me about her day at the bank. She said a very suspicious-looking man had walked in with a big black briefcase and everybody was sure he had a gun in there and was going to hold up the bank. Mom was ready to step on the alarm button on the floor, but then he opened the briefcase and took out a bunch of bottles of perfume he wanted to sell to the tellers. The story gave me the shivers. Two years ago there was a holdup in another bank in New Madison and one of the tellers was shot and killed. I kept thinking it might have been my mother.

Then she said, "I hear water running somewhere, don't you?" I listened, and I did hear a sound like water gurgling. Mom went upstairs to check, but came right back down saying she couldn't find anything running up there and she'd better check the basement and the garage.

In another minute she was back in the kitchen, her face as red as if she'd just come back from a couple of months on the beach. "Who left the hose on in the garage?" she asked.

"Not me," I said.

Just then, my father walked in. "Not me what?" he asked, looking worn out from his trip to Philadelphia, wrinkled, sweaty, and ready for something very cold to drink.

He kissed my mother and said, "Whew, hot," and then he patted my shoulder and asked, "Not me what?" again.

Mom said, "Wait till you see the garage, Don," and Dad said, "What happened in the garage?" and he and I ran down to look. Obviously Richard had left the hose running, not full blast, but just enough to flood the garage with about an inch of water in the couple of hours since he'd left.

"It's just not like Richard," my father kept saying while he and my mother were lying in wait for him.

"I don't understand how he could have been so careless," my mother said.

Of course, I knew exactly how he could. Anybody with his mind on stashing stolen musical instruments under his bed was capable of doing a lot of crazy things. I was sort of scared of what they'd do to him, since the flood had made a real mess down there and soaked through a couple of cartons of old clothes my mother was planning to give to the church—not to mention wetting some tools and the lawnmower. I quickly said, "But he did a good job on the car, didn't he?" and I think that saved him.

When Richard came home, Dad was angry. But although his voice sounded stormy, he managed to keep the high winds out of his lecture. He said some words to Richard that I hardly ever hear him use, like "irresponsible" and "thoughtless.' Then he said he hoped it would never happen again.

Richard is funny about certain things. If Mom screams at him, even when she really lets fly, he lets it roll off him like light rain. But if Dad so much as says words like "carelessness" or "misbehavior" to him, he goes up to his room and closes the door and doesn't come out again until a week from Tuesday.

That's what happened after Dad's lecture; Richard went to his room and stayed there until dinnertime. At dinnertime he came downstairs, ate his veal cutlet, and went right up again. I wasn't sure whether he was upset or just going up to guard the guitar.

When I went to my own room to go to bed I noticed it right away. My swim goggles were on my dresser where I'd left them, but the two dollars I'd left lying right next to them were gone.

FOUR

I stormed straight into Richard's room, ready to really let him have it, but the minute I stepped over the threshold I stopped in my tracks. Richard was lying on his bed, bunched up in the corner under his broken kite, with his eyes closed. He looked strange lying there in all his clothes, as if he'd fallen down and didn't want to bother getting up.

When I walked in, he opened his eyes halfway but didn't move.

"My two dollars are gone," I said, but although I intended to make my voice blast out of my mouth like a fire siren, I sounded more like my English teacher, Mrs. Melrose, who talks in squeaks that sound as if she went to Mouse University.

Richard still didn't move, but what I'd said was sinking in. I could see the way his nostrils opened wide and his eyebrows kind of moved up.

"I bet your friend stole them," I said, letting my eyes wander under his bed. I was mad enough to blurt out that I knew he was hiding stolen stuff, but something stopped me.

"You'll get them back," Richard said after a pause, and then he added, "tomorrow," and he rolled over and turned his face to the wall.

I'd come prepared for a big fight, and now, having won so quickly, I just stood there, not knowing what to do.

Richard solved that problem right away. "Can't you see I'm trying to sleep?" he said, meaning, "Get Out." So I turned and was just walking out the door when my eye fell on something on Richard's desk. A stamped envelope.

A letter? Richard is not much of a correspondent, and when he was away at camp year before last I remember how upset Mom was because he only managed to write two postcards in eight weeks. So what prompted him to write a letter now, and to whom?

I took a very quick look; touching anything on my brother's desk is as hazardous as tight-rope walking without a net, and I don't like to live dangerously.

The letter was sealed into an envelope and already had a stamp glued on and it was addressed to Mr. David Searles, New Mexico.

I guess Richard suddenly realized I was still in the room because he flipped over on his bed and opened his eyes and said, "Hey, buzz off, Snoopo!" and I said, "That will never get to your father if you don't even have a town or street or zip code or anything!" and Richard sat up and looked as if he might take off one of his shoes and throw it at me.

"But I don't blame you for trying," I said, and I ran out before anything flew in my direction.

The next day Mrs. Covelli called and asked me if I would take care of her cat, Aunt Agnes, while the Covellis went up to Cape Cod. I've been taking care of Aunt Agnes since I was nine, and she and I are really good friends. I know exactly where she likes to be scratched and when she's in the mood to play with her catnip toys, and what time she expects her dinner.

After lunch I went over to the Covellis' to pick up their house key. Mrs. Covelli put it into a yellow envelope so I wouldn't get it mixed up with any other keys. Then she drew a cat's face on the envelope. "I don't want to write my name or address on it," she explained. "This way, if by chance you should lose it, no one will know what house the key belongs to—but *you'll* know it's for Aunt Agnes."

Mrs. Covelli offered me some lemonade, and I drank it out of one of the cut-glass goblets that had belonged to her grandmother. Mrs. Covelli likes old things, and her house is full of stuff that looks as if it's going to fall apart if you sneeze—chairs you wouldn't dare sit on, lamps with china bases that would probably crack if you talked too loud, and silver bowls whose bottoms would fall out if you tried to put a marshmallow in them. These are antiques so valuable they belong in glass boxes in a museum, so when I go in to feed Aunt Agnes, I practically don't breathe if I'm not in the kitchen. As much as I like Mrs. Covelli, I was glad when I'd finished my lemonade and could set the goblet on the drainboard next to the sink. I wouldn't want to be the one to break a goblet that had maybe been hanging around since Abraham Lincoln was in third grade.

Mrs. Covelli watched me put the yellow envelope with the key in my pocket. "I always feel that Aunt Agnes is in good hands when we go away," she said, which made me feel really good. I don't mind the money I get paid, but I like the job even better.

Then she said, "I'll leave a light burning in the upstairs hall, and please be careful not to lose the key, Carolyn!" which is what she says every year.

"I'll be careful. Have a nice vacation!" I said, and that's what *I* say every year.

When I got home, I put the key in its envelope where I keep my locker and house keys, on my desk under the digital clock I got for Christmas. As I was leaving my room, Richard called me from downstairs. "Flim-flam's here. He's got something for you!"

I don't know what Richard said to Flim, but I noticed that the guitar was gone from under my brother's bed, Richard was looking at me in an almost friendly way, and Flim-flam was actually smiling in my direction. "A mistake, Carrie," he said, handing me my two dollars. "Sorry, kid."

Nobody calls me Carrie, but I sort of like it. "It's okay," I said. "Forget it. Square business." It was no mistake but I was glad to have my two dollars back.

Then he offered me a Lifesaver—not grape, but fortunately I like lime, too. "Thanks," I said.

"We're going to the club. Want a ride over?" Flim asked. Now that was really something. I'd never been invited in Flim's car before, not even for a drive around the block. "Sure," I said, but almost as soon as the car turned the corner, I realized it would have been a lot safer to take my bike the way I usually do. Flim-flam stuck a pot pipe in his mouth, lit up, and we were off. He whapped his foot on the gas pedal to make it shoot ahead, then whapped it down on the brake just to see us jerk forward in our seats. The car was so old it had no seat belts in the back, and one of the door handles was missing, too. When Flim-flam turned a corner, the car flew around the bend as if someone had spread margarine on the street. I thought any minute I might fly out through the door or the windshield.

Of course, I didn't let on. Richard seemed pretty scared, too, but he sort of laughed to let Flim-flam know he was no cream puff, and he yelled, "Floor it!" So I tried acting brave too, and said, "Yeah, floor it!" when what I really wanted to say was "Lemme outta here!" Of course, that was the stupidest thing I could have said because then Flim really slammed down on the gas pedal and we zoomed through two red lights and one full stop sign, screeching up and down the streets like in TV car chases.

Then, just as we turned into the club driveway, the old, broken glove compartment flew open. Flim-flam's hand shot out right away to shut it, but not before I'd caught sight of something sinister gleaming in there, under what looked like car-polishing rags. Maybe the speed of the car had given me a quick case of brain fever, but I thought I saw a knife blade. I held my breath waiting to see if Richard would say anything, but all he said was that he was in a hurry to get to the club to get some locker-painting jobs lined up so he could make some money. After a minute, I thought maybe I'd seen wrong or imagined it.

Anyway, I was so glad to have arrived at the club at all that I just raced to the locker, put on my bathing suit, and headed for the pool to try out my new swim goggles.

I swam around for about fifteen minutes, enjoying the way my goggles let me keep my eyes open under water without getting stung by the chlorine. Then Sarah Duwhinney asked if she could try them out. While she was using them I decided to do a few dives from the high board. I had lined up to take my turn when my ear caught a conversation that two mothers were having while they were watching their kids in the pool. One of them said, "I haven't reported it because I can't be sure I didn't lose it."

The other one said, "How much was in the purse?"

The first mother said, "About five dollars. I'd just spent

fifteen dollars at the five-and-ten and had the change from a twenty. Of course, it might have dropped out of my pocketbook on the street. I'm sure no one at the club would break into my *locker*. We've been members here for so many years—why, we know practically everyone here."

The second mother—and I now glanced over my shoulder and realized it was Mrs. Lovitt, one of Mom's good friends—said, "Was anything else missing?"

The first woman I now recognized as Mrs. Strawheim, whose locker is only four doors from ours, and what she said made my heart do a somersault in my chest. "Only one other thing. A little flashlight I carry in my purse with me so I can see to fit my key in my lock at night. It looks like a silver pen."

It's all I heard, but it was enough to ruin my dive and my day. I climbed the ladder to the twenty-foot board, my feet wobbling on each step. The penlight I'd seen in Richard's room, stolen from Mrs. Strawheim, who happened to be a very nice lady who was expecting a baby and who once lent me a dime when I didn't have change to call home and tell Mom I'd be late for dinner. And even if she hadn't been a very nice lady, she was someone we actually *know*. Maybe Richard hadn't taken it out of her locker himself, but he had it at home, on *his* desk. How much different is keeping stuff that's been stolen from actually stealing it yourself? Not much.

I had to hang on to the railings with all my force to keep myself steady. I got to the top, shaking like a sunfish sail in the wind, afraid I might just topple off the side of the board and smash into bits at the side of the pool. I wobbled to the end of the board and waited, wishing I could just turn around, walk off the board, down the steps and head straight home. But there were kids lined up behind me, getting impatient. I was in no mood for diving, but I had to go through with it anyway. I bounced up and down, lifted my arms, and went springing off the board.

I soared for a split second and then knew I'd done it all wrong—swooped when I should have arched, leaped when I should have stretched. *WHAP.* I hit the water flat, smack on my stomach and thighs—*OWCH!* A belly flop to end all belly flops. It hurt like crazy and I got my nose full of water besides. When I surfaced, Mrs. Strawheim was standing anxiously at the edge of the pool. "Carolyn, are you all right, dear?"

Right next to her was Mrs. Lovitt, who said, "That must have hurt, Carolyn. Really *hurt*."

It did, I thought. *It really did.*

FIVE

When I went to the Deck later for lunch, Richard was sitting at a white table under a sun umbrella all by himself, just staring at nothing. The Deck is a place where kids can buy hot dogs and sodas when they don't eat in the big club dining room with their parents.

"What are you doing?" I asked.

"I'm figure skating. What does it look like I'm doing? Boy, you ask some creaky questions. I'm sitting here, is what I'm doing."

"I thought you were going to get a job painting lockers."

"Against club rules. Mr. Prisco wouldn't let me."

Mr. Prisco is the club manager. He is very bald. The kids say hair is afraid to grow on his head—he's that tough. Also, they say if he grew hair he wouldn't be able to see out of the eyes at the back of his head. He does seem to know everything that goes on.

"Where did Flim-flam go?" I asked.

"Swimming."

"Are you sure?"

"Who's looking for him, Lyle the Crocodile?"

"Richard, Mrs. Strawheim is missing a penlight and five dollars out of her locker!"

Richard looked at me funny for a minute, but I couldn't tell if he wasn't a bit surprised or was pretending not to be a bit surprised. "Should we call the FBI?"

"Where's Flim-flam?" I asked again. Was he busy breaking into other lockers at this very minute? And how did he open Mrs. Strawheim's locker in the first place?

"Will you ever learn to M.Y.O.B.? He's at the pool."

"What are you going to do about that penlight and the money?" I wanted to know, and saw that my knowing surprised him. I could tell by Richard's face that I was never going to get an answer. I could also tell that he wasn't even thinking about the penlight and the money. Then it hit me. Richard was miserable because Flim-flam had gone swimming with Cookie.

"Do you want me to have lunch with you?" I asked, not that I really felt sorry for him. I kept seeing that silver flashlight every time I closed my eyes. I even saw it when my eyes were wide open. Still, Richard was having enough problems. I decided to drop the subject for now.

"I'm not hungry," Richard said.

"You haven't eaten *anything*?" I asked.

"Just two slices of pizza, a hot dog, a Coke, and two chocolate cupcakes."

"Two chocolate cupcakes! Dad would kill you."

"What about you stuffing up with Heavenly Hash?"

"Dad would kill us both."

Then Richard said something that really surprised me. "He's not *my* dad," he said.

I didn't know what to say, but I said, "What's the difference?" which came out sounding pretty stupid.

"Plenty," Richard said. I thought about it and guessed he was right, more or less. There is something peaceful about knowing both your parents and just where you came from and who you might take after—although my mother keeps telling me I take after my Uncle Paul in North Dakota, someone I only met once, when I was about three years old.

Richard looks like my mother, people tell him, but he has dark hair, and both Mom and Dad have lightish hair. In fact, Dad's tends to be reddish in summer and curls up near the hairline in humid weather, just like mine does, and when everyone in the family is together, Richard does look a little bit like he doesn't belong. Lately he's gotten very tall, too, and Mom said she noticed that his voice is really going bass, like his father's.

I don't think it should matter. My friend Jen looks nothing at all like either of her parents and it doesn't bother *her*. And another friend at school who is adopted says she never thinks about her real parents. She says your real parents are the people who've brought you up, spent all those mornings, noons, and nights of all those years watching you turn from a baby into a person.

That makes a lot of sense, but I didn't know exactly how to explain it to Richard. Not that he ever listens to anything I say anyway.

"I'm going to have a hot dog" is what I said instead, "and some fries."

"You might as well get me one, too," Richard said. "And another Coke. I'm thirsty."

I got on line for our food, and sure enough, from where I was standing I could see Flim-flam and Cookie just coming out of the pool. Stealing flashlights, money—and now trying to steal Richard's girlfriend! Now maybe Richard would feel Flim-flam was going too far and stop being friends with him.

Mom asked Richard at least once a week why he didn't invite some other kids over once in a while, and occasionally Richard showed up with this or that kid, but Richard is shy and probably likes Flim-flam because Flim acts big and takes charge. Flim-flam has what Richard calls "brass." Once he told my mother, "He makes things move."

"Out of lockers" is what I could add now. I put the paper tray with our hot dogs in front of Richard on the table, but Flim had gotten there first and dropped his drippy, sopping self into my chair. Immediately he reached over and snatched two of my French fries. Richard grabbed his wrist like a shot. "Those are my sister's, put 'em back," he said and Flim dropped the fries one-two-three, said, "Soooo soooorrry, Mother," and said he might as well go watch Cookie at diving practice. He took off fast.

As I said, Richard is not a bad kid.

"Thanks," I said, and Richard said, "Eat and don't talk." That's when I made up my mind that if only for my brother's sake, and even if I couldn't give back the five dollars right away, I'd return the flashlight to Mrs. Strawheim as soon as possible.

"As soon as possible" turned out to be after dinner that night. My parents were going to the discount store to see if they could buy a new redwood table for the patio and asked Richard and me if we wanted to come along. Richard said he was waiting for Flim-flam to come by with his new cassette, and I said I wanted to stay home to watch a rerun of "Galactica." What I really wanted to watch was Flim-flam, to make sure he didn't steal anything. Even more important was staying home to make sure that Flim-flam didn't get Richard to hide anything else he stole.

But Flim-flam arrived without the cassette. And something else was different. His hair was slicked down, and he wasn't wearing his usual dirty jeans. He was wearing white cotton pants and a new-looking T-shirt with the words "Imitation T-shirt" on it. For once, he didn't smell of pot; he smelled of shampoo. "Came by to tell you I can't stay tonight, Mother," he said to Richard, and he looked funny, as if he was going to say something else but then decided not to.

"Did you bring the tape at least?" Richard asked.

Flim-flam scratched his chin and looked even funnier. Not so much funny as guilty, actually. Seeing Flim-flam look guilty about something was a new experience. "No," he said.

"Hey, why not?" Richard asked. He'd been so busy drinking a can of orange soda Mr. Covelli had given him for helping transplant a little tree that he hadn't noticed the way Flim was edging toward the door.

"We'll listen to it another night, okay? I'm busy tonight."

"Busy? Where are you going?" Richard asked.

Then Flim said, "To Cookie's." At first Richard's expression didn't change and I thought he hadn't heard, but then he gulped a little gulp, and said, "Okay, see ya," and Flim-flam said, "See ya," and he left, zooming up the street like it was the Minneapolis Four Hundred.

After a minute I said, "He's some friend," and Richard looked as if he was going to take the half-empty orange soda can and crush it in his bare hands like it was a paper cup. "M.Y.O.C.B.," he said, and I asked, "What does the C stand for?" and Richard said, "Creaky!" and he turned on his heel and slammed out the back door.

SIX

It was still light out, and as good a time as any. I'd take the penlight over to the club and slip it under Mrs. Strawheim's locker door. Easy as pie when it got darker and the place cleared out. Mr. Prisco was not likely to be hanging around at night either.

I went up to Richard's room and found the penlight in his desk drawer, being very careful not to disturb anything. While I was up there, I took another look around, peeked into his closet, checked under the bed, and even took a quick look in a box on his night table. Nothing but a lot of old junk: a key from the Hotel Delano where we'd stayed one year on vacation, a bunch of Mexican coins Dad had brought back after his trip to a convention in Mexico City, rubber bands, ticket stubs from a rock concert, and that old birthday card Richard's real father had sent him like a hundred years ago. A bunch of nothing, and that was a relief—I was half expecting to find I-don't-know-what stolen stuff up there.

I tiptoed out, feeling like a cat burglar myself, and stuck the penlight in the pocket of my jeans. Then I went to the kitchen, helped myself to a little dish of Heavenly Hash for stamina, washed it down with fresh-fruit crush (Dad likes me to drink a lot of that stuff because he says it's natural and very healthy) and off I went on my bike.

By the time I got to the club it was almost dark. Good. I chained my bike to the bike rack and was about to head for the lockers when I realized that one of the other two or three bikes chained there was Richard's.

Richard's bike? What was he doing here at night all by himself? Seeing his bike gave me a big scare. He sure wasn't here to play tennis in the dark, he wasn't here to sun himself on the beach, and he wasn't here to paint the floor of our locker. The Deck was closed by this time, too. In fact, nobody was around.

I shouldn't have eaten that Heavenly Hash; it was making my stomach hurt even more than it did the day I took the belly flop. I was scared I'd find Richard with Flim-flam after all, helping him pry open locker doors and go through other people's pocketbooks, satchels, beach bags. For a long time I just stood there next to his bike, waiting for the high tide in my stomach to die down. I was afraid to go to the lockers, not knowing what I'd find there, and I was afraid not to go.

Finally I tiptoed into the first row of lockers—our row—and stopped every four steps to listen for sounds. Now it was dark and I was spooked, like the time I made the mistake of going into the Fun House at the amusement park because I thought it would be fun. It was full of green ghouls that popped screaming out of black corners just when you were looking at a horror skeleton in the other direction or ducking a bloody severed head that flew past your own face from overhead. That was no fun, and this was no fun, either.

I inched along to our row and stood there listening to a big, heavy silence. At any moment I expected one of the locker doors to creak open and to see something I didn't want to see.

Then I remembered why I'd come. I had the penlight stuck in my pocket and had only to slip it under the door of Mrs. Strawheim's locker, number 114, and disappear. Easy. Then I'd just get back on my bike and fly home like the wind. If Richard wanted to get into trouble here, it wasn't my business; I'd get out, zip, and pretend I'd never seen his bike. In fact, I'd pretend I'd never been here at all.

I crept along, my heart going under my T-shirt. You would have thought *I* was the criminal the way I was sneaking along, imagining noises, keeping close to the locker doors, and groping my way past numbers 111, 112, 113 . . . . I stopped. What if Mrs. Strawheim was in there, quietly waiting to see if she could catch the thief trying to lift something else? What if the door flew open and, worse, *Mr.* Strawheim appeared, grabbed me by the shirt, and nailed me to the wall?

Silly. Nobody sat around in the dark in lockers, waiting for crooks.

I heard a sound. Or did I imagine it? I froze, waiting. I heard it again. A gaspy, funny noise, coming from somewhere. From where? Not from the lockers, but from somewhere close.

Gurgles. Unearthly sploshy, whooshy sounds. Worse than the sound effects in the Fun House. The sounds were coming from the swimming pool! I crept through the dark passages between the lockers, making my way to the wire pool gate. I walked along the wooden planky floor, my footsteps sounding as if they were being broadcast on a public-address system—and finally I turned the last corner leading to the wire gate and stood facing the swimming pool.

During the day, it glows blue and green and shines as if the maintenance crew had dumped a ton of emeralds to the bottom. But now, at night, the green had turned to a spook-black shimmer, and because there were clouds covering the moon, the whole place was like some weird Martian landscape.

At the deep end a figure clung to the side, his arms glistening against the rim of the pool as if someone had greased them, his wet hair catching what little light there was. I couldn't see his face at first but knew for sure whose it was—Richard's. I could hear his raspy breathing cutting through the silence, and now he was letting go of the side of the pool and beginning to struggle in the water, gasping and gurgling, and spurting water out of his mouth.

Richard in the deep end of the pool? I was terrified. He kept sinking under and then bobbing up again; his whole body was jerking in the water as if it were motorized.

And his head went down again! It was gone, under the black water and out of sight!

I couldn't open the gate. It was, of course, locked. Richard must have climbed over it. Well, if he could, I could. But as I was nearly at the top, one of my sneakers jammed into a space between the gate and the fence. I was stuck! But it was only for a split second—I twisted my foot, freed my sneaker, leaped down like Wonder Woman, and flew to the deep end of the pool. I stood at the edge, and my breathing nearly stopped. Had he gone off his cork to try to learn to swim in the deep end of the pool at night when there was no lifeguard within fifty miles to save him when he sank to the bottom? Had he completely lost his mind to think that jerking his arms and legs was going to keep him from sinking like a bag of rocks?

He bobbed up again and his arms flew up over his head, he

took a breath, and for a moment I saw one shoulder come up before his face sank again. I screamed, "Richard!"—but of course his ears were under the water, too, and he didn't hear me.

I guess I went a little crazy myself; I ripped off my sneakers and I just leaped in, with my jeans and T-shirt and everything still on, and I lunged at my brother in the water. He grabbed my arm as if it were a floating log and nearly dragged me down with him, but I pushed him off long enough to breathe and tried to remember what they'd taught us about lifesaving in swimming class. I never took the lifesaving course (you had to be sixteen at our club), but I knew you were supposed to sort of grab the victim around the neck and pull him nicely behind you. It wasn't going to work here—Richard was bobbing and jerking and sinking and grabbing and gasping, and it was all I could do to keep out of the way of his arms. So I reached for his trunks in the back to give me something to hold on to and dragged him a few feet until I could reach the edge of the pool and hang on there. Once I got to the side, I was gasping for air myself. But I still had Richard's swim trunks in my fist, and I pulled him toward me. He grabbed frantically for the edge and sputtered all over me.

"Are you crazy?" I said. I said it maybe ten times, while he just hung there by his elbows, gulping in air.

Finally, he lifted himself out of the water and lay at the edge of the pool, stretched out and breathing hard like a corpse just brought back to life. I pulled myself out of the water, too, and said, "Are you crazy?" one more time, in case he hadn't heard the other ten times.

Then I just sat there shivering, my wet clothes sticking all over me, feeling as if I'd just gone through a car wash in January.

When Richard started breathing like a normal person, I said, "What were you *doing*?" and Richard said, "Reciting the Pledge of Allegiance. What did it *look* like I was doing?"

"Drowning. You were drowning."

"Drowning! Are you kidding? I was teaching myself how to swim is what I was doing. And you didn't have to jump into the pool like some creaky lifeguard out to save her quota of lives. And now I suppose you're gonna tell everybody in our time zone that you rescued me from a watery grave, huh?"

He rolled his head over to look at me, and maybe it was just that his face was still wet or maybe it was that it was too dark to see things right, but I could swear that a tear came out of his right eye and went running down his cheek.

"I'm not going to tell anybody," I said, and I added, "Mister Grateful," and Richard rolled his head back and just stared up at the sky, as if there were something up there to see.

Right now there actually was. The clouds had parted and we could see the moon. It was nice—not quite round, but almost, as if someone had sat on it and flattened it a bit on one side, and it was a gorgeous color, almost like a ball of silver foil. It got us quiet, just looking up, as if someone had hung a "Do Not Disturb" sign in the sky.

Finally, Richard sat up and said, "I guess I'll call it quits for tonight," and I saw him shiver, too. I wanted to make him promise he'd never come out here at night again, never go into a pool without someone there to watch, but I didn't say it. It probably wasn't necessary anyway. As I watched him pull on his shirt, I had the feeling he wouldn't try this again, ever.

I got up, picked up my sneakers, and headed for the gate, and all of a sudden Richard was next to me and he did something weird. He put his arm around my shoulder and kissed the side of my head over my ear. He hasn't done that since Mom practically held a gun to his back at my eighth birthday party the time Dad was trying out the new movie camera.

It took me by absolute complete surprise. When I recovered, I said, "Yuk," and Richard said, "Carolyn Frankfurter"—just to remind me, I guess, of what could happen if I ever opened my mouth to tell a soul.

"I'll race you home," I said.

SEVEN

The next day my mother found the penlight. It was the day Mr. and Mrs. Covelli left for Cape Cod, and I was feeding Aunt Agnes and trying to get her interested in a catnip mouse, when I heard Mom calling me. I figured it was time to set the table for dinner, so I ambled back to our house.

My mother was scooping seeds out of a melon, and she looked over her shoulder when I came into the kitchen. "Oh, there you are, Carolyn. I thought you were upstairs. Is that yours?" she said, pointing her chin in the direction of the kitchen table.

The penlight! All forgotten the night of the big dunk. I'd never taken it out of my jeans pocket and, come to think of it, since it flew into the pool along with me, it couldn't be in working order anyway. Still, just seeing it lying there turned my tongue into a big hunk of wood in my mouth.

"I found it on the floor of the laundry room," Mom said and went back to scooping away, without a care in the world.

Last night after Richard and I had raced home, I'd thrown my wet jeans and T-shirt into the dryer, and probably the penlight fell out onto the floor. Until now, I hadn't given it a thought.

"Not mine," I said, and I ran outside again so she wouldn't stop scooping melon seeds and examine my face. She has a way of reading my mouth even when I don't say anything.

I ran outside and sat on the patio looking at the knocked-down pieces of our new picnic set, hoping Richard would come home so I could warn him. On second thought, I couldn't do that, since then he'd know that I'd taken it out of his room, and so on.

Last night, Dad had brought the picnic table and benches home in a few cartons and proceeded to try putting them all together, which for Dad turned out to be like climbing a glass mountain. Especially, as Dad kept saying in his keep-the-lid-on-it voice, since the screws were too big for the holes, the whole thing was put together by clowns, and the directions were written free-style by chimpanzees. Also, he did not have the right size screwdriver. Richard had an assignment today: to buy the largest available screwdriver at Main Street Hardware.

That's probably where Richard was now; he'd gone back to the club first thing this morning after phoning Cookie and making a date to play tennis at eleven. I overheard him talking to her as I stood behind the dining room door eating a healthful carrot, which is supposed to improve your eyesight but wasn't hurting my hearing, either. I'd also heard Richard phone Flim-flam to say he couldn't see him today.

But Richard didn't come home until we were all at the table about to put our spoons into our melons, and then he raced in, red in the face, washed up, and dashed to his place at the table.

I sat on the edge of my chair waiting for Mom to whip out the penlight and shine it into his face and demand to know where he'd gotten it, and I expected a volcano scene during which Richard either fainted or confessed all; but although we did have a scene, it wasn't what I expected.

First there was the usual talk about "What did you do today?" and "Did you have a good day at the bank?"—the ordinary back-and-forth. Then Dad asked Richard how he'd spent the day and Richard said he'd been at the club. So Dad asked if the floor of our locker had ever gotten painted, and the answer from Richard was that no, he'd forgotten about it and anyway he didn't think it needed painting very badly now and it would be better to wait until the end of the season when no one was going to walk all over it, but Dad did not agree. Fall, he said, would be too late, and the leaves would stick to it, and then Dad asked who'd left the empty orange-soda can lying around on the patio last night, and the way he said "orange soda" sounded like the way I say "worms and snakes."

"I guess I left it there," Richard said, and I could tell Dad didn't like his leaving it there, didn't like the casual way that he said he'd left it there, and didn't like the fact that he drank orange soda in the first place.

"Where'd you get it, anyway?" Dad asked, and by his voice I knew he'd had a bad day.

Richard said that Mr. Covelli had given it to him, and Dad said although a can of orange soda wasn't going to hurt anyone now and then, it would be better to drink just about anything else, and although Mr. Covelli might not know enough to watch his diet, Dad looked into people's mouths every day, saw the results of too much sugar from morning till night, read all the scientific studies, and hoped that we'd learn from his experience and stop stuffing up with junk.

When the lecture was over and I thought we could go on to eat our hamburgers peacefully, Dad took a big breath and, as if now that his motor was charged up, he was going to make use of its momentum, said to Richard, "Did you get the screwdriver?"

Richard put his fork down and got an "oops" look on his face and shook his head no.

Then Dad put his fork down and said, "No?" and Mom sighed. I sort of tried to get ready for what was coming.

"How come?" Dad said. He got those lines over his forehead that look like sheet music before someone puts in the musical notes.

Richard said, "I forgot," and Dad said, "You *forgot*?" like it was an echo off the side of a mountain.

Richard nodded.

"But you knew I was going to work on the picnic table tonight, Richard."

Richard looked as if he'd lost his taste for dinner. "I'll go buy one right now," he said, getting up.

Dad said, "You can't go now. The hardware store isn't open at night." Richard sat down again.

Dad shook his head and let out a big sigh, and I think that was a mistake. It was worse than any words he could have said to Richard. It sounded as if he was saying, "You are a no-good disappointment who never does a thing right." Maybe, to Richard, it even sounded like "If you were my own flesh-and-blood kid, you would have remembered to buy the screwdriver."

Richard made a mistake, too. He should have said, "I'm sorry I forgot, Dad," but he didn't. Instead he got up from the table with a cut-down look, said "I'm not hungry," and went right up to his room.

Mom pushed the food around on her plate without putting anything into her mouth, and we were all very quiet for a couple of minutes. Then Dad asked her if she thought he'd been too stern with Richard and Mom said no, that Dad had every right to be annoyed; Richard was not doing much with his time this summer and should have certainly remembered to do the one little errand Dad had asked him to.

Then, after a few minutes, Dad got up and went to the foot of the stairs and called "Richard!" a couple of times. I heard Richard open the door to his room, and Dad called up, "Would you like to shoot baskets after dinner?" and Richard said, "No, thanks. I'm pretty tired," and I heard his door close again.

I hadn't heard Dad ask Richard to shoot baskets in a long time, and I was surprised Richard turned him down; Richard loves basketball.

Dad came back to the table and he said, "I don't know what's wrong with the kid, he doesn't seem to be motivated to do anything. Wouldn't you think he'd at least try to learn to *swim*?"

I opened my mouth to tell them how Richard had nearly drowned trying to teach himself, and remembered just in time to close it again. I did ask, "How come he didn't learn when he was little, like I did?" But I've asked that a million times and no one's ever given me a real answer.

This time my mother said, "It was just one of those things, Carolyn. Richard was always scared of the water. Please clear the table." Suddenly I got really annoyed. Just one of those things? One of *what* things?

I carried out the dishes and scraped them and rinsed them and stuck them into the dishwasher, and I knew that there were things my mother wasn't telling me and things she wasn't telling Richard. Richard was always scared of the water—why? *I* was never scared of water. I am scared of electricity because once when I was little I tried to stick a ballpoint pen into a wall socket and I got a bad shock. Did Richard get some sort of real scare in the water?

I was so involved thinking about all this that I got careless and let a saucepan lid fly out of my soapy hand. It clattered to the kitchen floor so loudly you'd have thought a crystal chandelier had fallen on the floor tiles.

"What was that?" my mother called from the dining room, and I called back, "It was just one of those things." I am not usually fresh, but sometimes it's absolutely necessary.

My mother was in the kitchen in a flash. "What kind of answer was that?" she demanded.

I was on the verge of saying, "Some remarks are just not meant for thirty-eight-year-old ears," but didn't dare.

I simply looked her right in the eye and asked her again why Richard is scared of water, and this time I guess she understood I was old enough to know. Maybe she thought I even let the lid clatter purposely, or that I'd turned from twelve to thirteen between dinner and cleanup. Anyhow, she didn't get mad.

"When Richard was just a toddler, his father tried to teach him to swim," she said. "And because he himself hadn't learned until he was almost twenty-five, he was determined that his son was going to learn early. Even before he could walk properly! That's how Richard's father was anyhow—a perfectionist about everything. He couldn't stand failure. Richard would stand in the shallow end and just splash and play and never make an effort to copy the strokes his father was trying to teach him. So his father took him to the deeper end, threw him in, and—" My mother shrugged, picked up a frying pan, and started to get very busy scraping the burned stuff out of the bottom. "So, of course, little Richard sank right to the bottom.

"His father pulled him right out, but now Richard was scared of the pool. That made David even more determined. He did it again the next day. Richard was even more scared. I tried to stop David, but he showed me an article in a magazine about an Olympic swimmer who had learned to swim in just exactly this way—by being thrown into deep water when he was even younger than Richard. It went on every day for I don't know how long, and it seemed to me that each time, Richard's father let him stay under a bit longer, hoping that Richard would have to save himself. It got to the point where Richard would scream when I took his bathing suit out of the bureau drawer. I finally got Richard's father to stop, but it was too late. Richard was so terrified of water that for a long time I couldn't even get him into the bathtub."

"Richard's father sounds mean," I said, and for a minute my mother didn't answer. Then she said, "Sometimes, in a way, he was. I think he was very unhappy and sort of took it out on us."

Now that I understood, I wanted to rush upstairs and make Richard understand, too. Maybe he remembered how it felt to open his mouth and gasp for air and feel the water rush into his nose and throat and lungs. Once at the Jersey shore a wave pulled me too far out, held me under the salty rush of water a few seconds too long. I remembered that now—how I couldn't get up to breathe, the pressure, my terror—and I really shivered, just remembering.

I went up to Richard's room and knocked on the door. "Richard, can I come in?" I said. No answer.

"Hey, Richard!" I called. No answer.

I pushed open the door a half-inch; the room was dark—and empty. I tiptoed over to the window to see if he might be down below in the backyard or in the driveway. No. At least, it was too dark out in the back to see anything, even with the lights shining from the Covellis' kitchen and basement windows.

The lights shining from the Covellis' kitchen and basement windows?

But Mrs. Covelli had told me clearly that she would keep a light burning only in the upstairs hall!

When I was over there earlier to feed Aunt Agnes, it was still daylight, and I hadn't even turned the lights on, so I know I didn't forget to shut them off. Someone was in there, right now!

I flew back to my room to get the Covellis' key so Dad could go right over there with me—or with the police. I went directly to my digital clock, lifted it, and reached for the yellow envelope with the cat's face on it.

There it was, just where I'd left it, next to my locker key. But it was empty. The Covellis' key was gone!

EIGHT

My heart was beating like ten drums. I flew down the stairs, barely feeling my sneakers touch the steps, and nearly collided with my mother, who was carrying iced tea out to my father on the screened porch.

"Where's Richard?" I said, barely getting the words out. The beats seemed to be moving from my chest into my mouth.

"Isn't he upstairs?" my mother asked.

"No. Where is he?"

"I don't know," my mother said. "I didn't see him leave. What did you want to borrow?" She smiled.

Of course, she hadn't seen him leave. He'd left secretly. Richard had sure as anything moved as silently as Aunt Agnes and had taken Mrs. Covelli's house key with him. Who else could have taken it between Aunt Agnes's dinner and ours? What else he was doing over at the Covellis' I could only—with extra drum/heartbeats—imagine.

I had to make a snap decision. Calling the police was out;

telling my father was in. This was serious. I was responsible for Mrs. Covelli's key, cat, and house, and Richard had absolutely no right to take the key without my permission, which I would never have given him. I began to march out to the screened porch to tell Dad but changed my mind when I remembered the scene Dad and Richard had had at dinner. I'd go right over to the Covellis' myself, first. To tell the truth, I didn't want another Dad-versus-Richard scene, not tonight, not ever.

"Maybe Richard's out in the yard," I said to Mom, and I did an about-face and headed out the front door.

I went directly to the driveway and stared at the Covellis' lit windows, and then I admit I got scared. Just suppose it wasn't Richard at all in there. Just suppose the key had slipped out of the envelope on my way home without my noticing it, and a thief had found the key and was now in there in a mask with a gun in his hand and extra bullets in his pocket.

Was I going to barge in there and maybe get tied up and shoved in a closet with a gag on my mouth or maybe get shot through the heart?

I went back into the house, panting and upset, and despite the possibility of a scene, I told Dad that the key to the Covellis' house was missing and that I thought Richard had taken it and that I was scared out of my wits and that the lights were on over there and would he come over there with me this minute?

My mother said, "That boy!" and shook her head and asked me if I was sure. Then Dad asked me to check my room one more time to make sure the key wasn't lying around on the floor or someplace. So I ran back to my room and checked the floor, the table, and my desk, and I went back downstairs and told Dad that the key was absolutely and certainly missing.

I followed Dad out as far as the driveway, and then he told me to stop and wait for him there. He went to the Covellis' back door and I saw him raise his fist to knock on the glass pane in the door, but then he tried the doorknob, and—sure enough—the door was open.

I guess Richard hadn't bothered to close the door behind him. I heard Dad yell "Richard!" into the house, and not even a minute later, I saw Richard appear in the glass door pane. His face looked like a wax mask that would crack if you touched it.

Dad pushed the door open, and he and Richard just stood there face to face for a minute. Then Dad's voice came out really low, as if he'd suddenly gotten an infection and didn't want to irritate the membranes in his throat. "What in heaven's name are you doing in there?" he asked Richard. It was more horrible than horrible, the way he said it. Too quiet. Like a cannon fuse, silently lit.

Richard's mask-face looked surprised. You'd think he had opened a door and found forty friends in a living room wishing him happy birthday.

Dad said it again, this time louder: *"What were you doing in here?"*

"Looking for a screwdriver," Richard said, and he held up his right hand, and sure enough, he was holding a big fat screwdriver. Mr. Covelli's.

For a minute, I guess Dad was at a loss for words. I suppose, after lighting the fuse, he'd been all prepared to fire the big cannon, and now he had no real reason to. Richard was only trying to help, right?

Sort of right. "You had no business going into the Covellis' house without permission," Dad said.

"You needed the screwdriver," Richard said. Definitely right, I thought.

"I said you should have asked permission. Your sister is responsible for the key and the Covellis' house."

"She wouldn't have given me permission," Richard said.

Also right. I would never have let Richard snoop around the Covellis' place when they weren't there.

"Then we would have done without the screwdriver," Dad said.

"You were the one who wanted it. You wanted to put the table together," Richard said. He handed the screwdriver to Dad.

"Thanks," Dad said, "but you were wrong to take the key, wrong to go into the Covellis' house, and wrong to have forgotten to buy me a screwdriver today in the first place."

Richard's mouth turned down at the corners. He looked Dad right in the eye and let his voice go even lower than Dad's, saying, "I guess you think everything I do is wrong." With that, he marched past Dad, handed me the Covellis' key, and ran into our house. A minute later I saw the light go on in his room.

Dad shook his head. "I can't seem to get through to that kid," he said, and he shrugged and walked over to the patio and began to put together the picnic table.

I noticed he did use the Covellis' screwdriver.

I also noticed that Mom had been standing at our own open kitchen door and had probably heard most of Dad and Richard's conversation. When I went into the kitchen for a glass of fruit crush, she was standing with her back to the sink staring down at the floor tiles. From the expression around her mouth I could tell she was having one of her back-of-the-head headaches.

I tried to cheer her up by changing the subject, telling her about Aunt Agnes, how she'd poke the toilet paper dispenser with her paw to watch it spin, but Mom wasn't listening. She kept her eyes glued to nothing in particular and finally, in the middle of one of my sentences, she said, "I'm worried about your brother."

I took some ice cubes out of the freezer and put them in my glass and I said, "Boy, I'm thirsty," because I didn't know what else to say.

"Richard gets his back up whenever your father corrects him, even when he's right and Richard's wrong. And I don't like the way Richard's behaving. I don't like his friends—" she meant Flim-flam, of course—"and I'm not happy about the way he spends his time."

It was as if she was thinking aloud and I was listening to a tape-recorded brain-reading.

I poured fruit crush in my glass and said, "I think he misses his own father," and one look at my mother's face convinced me I should never have let that slip out. I tried to make it all right by telling her Dad was really great, but Richard probably just once wanted to meet his real dad. Mom listened, and then she completely surprised me by agreeing with me.

And then she nearly floored me by saying that meeting his own father might be exactly the right thing for Richard and that she would try to arrange it.

"You mean you know where he *is*?" I asked, practically choking on my mouthful of crush.

My mother looked thoughtful. "I have an old address. I could write to him. If he's moved, maybe they'll forward the letter."

I tried to picture Richard's father in my mind and imagined someone very tall and sort of dark. I imagined him taking out a pair of glasses to read the letter from Mom, pictured him sitting at his desk, lifting his pen to write a reply, then saw him pasting a stamp on the envelope and running to the mailbox to get the letter in the slot before the next mail pickup.

"Carolyn," my mother was saying, interrupting my daydream, "I think it's better not to say anything to Richard. I mean, about my writing the letter. All right, dear?"

I understood. If the letter couldn't be forwarded, it would be too disappointing for Richard. Even worse, if his father did get the letter but didn't reply—wow!—Richard might just stay in his room until the end of time.

"Okay," I said.

About half an hour later, when I was up in my room, I heard Dad come up the stairs and knock on Richard's door. If I open the medicine cabinet in the bathroom and put my ear real close, I can usually catch the drift of any conversation in Richard's room. I flew to the bathroom and opened the cabinet, trying not to let it squeak. Dad was saying, "Listen, Rich, want to come down and have a rap at our new picnic table? It leans to the left a bit and I wouldn't try to stand an elephant on it, but I think I got it put together strong enough to hold a few hamburgers."

I heard Richard mumble something. Then Dad said, "You sure?" and a minute later, I heard him leave Richard's room and walk downstairs with slow, tired steps.

It was more than I could stand. I started for Richard's room, but on the way my eye caught something lying on the little table at the top of the stairs, the one where Mom always dumps the socks that don't match when she brings up the laundry. The penlight! Mom must have carried it up with the laundry and absent-mindedly left it lying there. I grabbed it, flicked the switch, and—miracle!—it still worked.

I threw open Richard's door, and just as I'd expected, there was my brother lying on his bed, face to the wall. "Dad was just trying to be nice," I said.

He spun around and glared at me and I aimed the flashlight beam right into his face.

"Where'd you get that?" Richard asked, glaring.

"You know it's Mrs. Strawheim's," I said, trying to sound good and tough and ready to blab everything I knew to the world. "Don't you have a *conscience*?" I asked.

"If Flim-flam took it, why should it be on *my* conscience?"

"'Cause he's *your* creaky friend!" I cried.

"Listen, will you stop using my words, wearing my shirts, and getting into my act?" Richard said, and he flipped back toward the wall so fast he made the kite over the bed wobble with the draft.

"Don't you know that creaky jerk is going to get you in trouble?" I asked, ignoring what he'd said.

"And if I get into trouble, what's it got to do with you?" he mumbled.

I put the flashlight on his desk. Suddenly I didn't feel so tough anymore. "I'll tell you what it's got to do with me," I said softly. "You're my brother, is what it's got to do with me."

"*Half*-brother," Richard reminded me, and hearing him say it made me feel as if I were hitting the water flat on my stomach again.

NINE

It was less than a week later, a Tuesday night, that the call came.

We were having a barbecue, and Dad was just about to slice the London broil when the telephone rang. As usual, I got sent in to answer it, even though, with both Jen and Barbara gone, I was sure the call wouldn't be for me. I grumbled a little because I was hungry and all ready to dive into my salad, but I did run inside and pick up the phone.

"Hello. Is this the Desmond residence?" a man's voice asked, and I said that it was. Then he said, "May I please speak to Rickie?" and I hesitated, because I'd never heard anyone call Richard "Rickie."

"You mean Richard?" I asked, and the man said, "Yes, please."

Very polite and ordinary. I thought it must be one of Richard's teachers or a neighbor asking him to help with yard work or someone like that. "Who's calling, please?" I asked, very routinely.

"Tell him his father is calling," the man said then, and I nearly dropped the phone. I guess I can blame my fuzzy mind on my empty stomach, but it had never occurred to me that the man on the other end could be Richard's father. For one thing, he sounded like he was calling from no further away than the Covellis', not from any faraway spot like New Mexico. For another thing, he sounded nice and pleasant, not like some mean man who would throw a little scared kid into the deep end of a pool and nearly let him drown.

"Just a minute, please," I said, in the most normal voice I could get out of my shocked and suddenly unfuzzed head. I stumbled out to the patio and delivered the message very calmly, as if I were telling everybody that the baked potatoes were ready but feeling as if I were announcing that the moon had fallen into the front yard.

The look on Richard's face: zero. It didn't sink in. He said, "Huh?" like it was a joke in Yugoslavian, and now would I please tell it again in English.

"Your father's on the telephone. He wants to speak to you." I said it again, slowly and clearly. I noticed Mom and Dad looking at each other with raised eyebrows.

Richard got up, letting his napkin slide to the floor. "My *father*?" he said, and I nodded. He started to move, but slowly. Maybe he thought this was a practical joke and he didn't want anybody to think he was really falling for it.

"Come *on*, it's long distance!" I said, and then he gathered speed and broke into a sort of running walk. He sped past me through the screen door and let it bang behind him.

I went to the table and started my salad, and my mother passed the bread basket to my father and said, "I hope I did the right thing," and my father said, "Maybe it was the only thing to do." Then there was a big nothing-to-say sort of lapse in the conversation. We sat there eating and listening to the crickets, and waiting.

We didn't have to wait long. Richard came back and picked up his napkin and folded it in his lap—which he usually has to be reminded to do—and then, believe it or not, he flashed a smile as if he'd just won the million-dollar state lottery.

"That *was* my father. He's coming to see me," he said, and if a genie had suddenly popped out of the ketchup bottle the three of us couldn't have been in a bigger state of shock.

When we had slightly recovered, my mother asked, "Coming here?" and my father asked, "To *our* house?" and I asked, "When?" You'd think this was our family dinner act and we'd rehearsed it.

"Yes. Here, to our house. Day after tomorrow," Richard said, like he was giving some ordinary piece of daily information, instead of this firecracker that practically had real sparks flying through the air of our yard.

It turned out that Richard's father was now traveling north regularly, had gotten Mom's letter (which had only said that Richard would like to meet him someday), and was already in Ohio and calling from a motel in Dayton. He'd make it to our house about four on Thursday.

For once, I couldn't read the expression on my mother's face. I guessed she was plenty shocked but trying not to show it. My father was suddenly pretending a great interest in the stuff on his plate so I couldn't read him either, but I did catch the light that seemed to be shining right out of Richard's eyes. It brightened up his whole face. He tore into his steak as if he hadn't eaten in days. He kept smiling and telling my mother the salad was really great tonight, and then he told Dad a joke he'd heard at the tennis courts at the club that afternoon. He even laughed hard at the joke himself and could barely get the punch line out. This was a new Richard.

After dinner, he helped clear the table and offered to scrape the grill with the wire brush, a really dirty job. When he said, "I think I'll get a haircut tomorrow, huh?" I had to hold on tight to my fork so it wouldn't fall out of my hand, and I saw Dad give Mom a look.

As I said, a new Richard.

After dinner, I actually got him to play a game of backgammon with me. Later I heard him talking on the telephone. He was asking Cookie to have a slice and a Coke with him at Rizzo's Pizzeria—this about an hour and a half after he'd eaten everything in sight at our barbecue. Before he left, he came into my room to listen to a record I'd been trying to get him to hear ever since I'd bought it before school closed.

While we were listening to my record together, a feeling came over me that's hard to explain. There was Richard sitting in my old wicker chair with the stuffed animals he'd taken off it actually on his lap, and I felt suddenly very warmed up by his being there. Sometimes I want to kick him or punch him, see him locked in a dungeon and put on bread and water for a couple of days, but now I guess I have to say it—I really loved him. I wished he would stay here in my room and never leave, that the record would go on and on, and that good moments like these could stretch on forever.

But as soon as the record was over, he jumped up.

"Don't you want to hear the other side?" I asked.

"Gotta run," Richard said. "Maybe tomorrow, okay?" He gave my arm a soft squeeze under the sleeve of my T-shirt (which used to be his T-shirt) on his way out the door. Then he turned in the doorway and said, "For a half-sister, you're not that bad. You're more like three-quarters, ho ho."

"Very funny," I said. Somehow I already knew that tomorrow and the whole bunch of other tomorrows following it could never be just like tonight.

Tomorrow: Richard, the new Richard, flew out of bed at nine o'clock. And for Richard, that is very early. Some days he doesn't rise and shine until the afternoon soap operas have gone on the air. Some days I've seen him in pajamas as late as three o'clock.

But today it was scrambled eggs for energy at nine-fifteen and ready for action at quarter of ten. First he was off to the barber shop, and after he came back, although it started to rain a little at about noon, he began sweeping the patio. He pushed the soppy broom around the patio and straightened out the new table and chairs and moved some plants this way and that way and wiped off my father's chaise longue and said that it was high time we got a new fiberglass awning. Then Flim-flam came by, but Richard sent him away. "Gotta get this place in shape. My father is coming tomorrow," he said, with waterdrops dripping off his face and hair.

I couldn't believe it.

Afterward, he checked the living room and moved the pillows on the couch so they'd cover the places that he thought were worn, and then he straightened the magazines on the coffee table.

"But he's not coming until *tomorrow*," I reminded him.

"Tomorrow I'll vacuum up the place and fix up the front yard," Richard said.

At four o'clock the doorbell rang, and we really jumped. Maybe he'd come a day early!

But it wasn't Richard's father, it was Cookie. She was holding a bunch of flowers she'd brought over from her own yard. "Since your father is coming, I thought you might want to stick these in a vase," she said. Her voice went up and down even more than usual. She seemed a little nervous, and I had the feeling that she'd brought the flowers as an excuse to see Richard. She sneezed. "Are you allergic to lilacs?" I asked.

"No, just to roses, but all flowers make me sneeze," she said.

"Me too," Richard said. He asked her in, and she said she'd help clean if he wanted her to, although the place looked clean enough already.

Richard said he was pretty well finished for today and he just wanted to wipe the dust off the window sills, and he offered Cookie a glass of fruit crush. Then he gave me a get-out-of-the-living-room look. I moved off to the screened porch. If I sit in the chair by the window wall and put my head against the paneling, I can pretty much hear what's being said in the living room.

Richard was telling Cookie about his father. "He was out of a job for a couple of years," he was saying, "but now he's sales manager of a big company. He's always traveling too, which is why I haven't seen a lot of him."

Cookie said that was really understandable.

"Of course, he sends me stuff now and then . . . although not a lot, 'cause he's a busy guy."

I put my head closer to the paneling.

"Now that he's with this great company, I wouldn't be surprised if they made him vice-president soon," Richard said.

Cookie said, "Wow."

"I wouldn't be surprised if he hadn't already bought himself a little Porsche or something. Now *there's* a car," Richard said.

"Gorgeous," said Cookie.

"Blue would be nice. I'll try to talk him into blue if he hasn't already bought one," Richard went on.

Cookie giggled. "I like silver," she said.

"Maybe he'll buy two," Richard said.

Too much! I jumped up and ran to the door of the living room and shot him an are-you-kidding look. I tried to make my eyes stare holes right through him. "Could I see you in the kitchen a minute?" I asked.

Richard looked back at me as if he wished I'd go up in a puff of green smoke, but with Cookie there he couldn't say much. He followed me into the kitchen and let me have it in big whispers. "Will you stop *spying* on me?" he croaked.

"Are you trying for the Wishful Thinking Award?" I asked.

"What are you talking about?" Richard said, but I saw that his lower lip was about to twitch the way it always does when he's really uncomfortable.

"Are you trying to flim-flam Cookie into believing all that made-up stuff about your father?" Right away I was sorry I asked that, because I could see from my brother's expression that he wasn't really trying to con Cookie that his father was great. He was only trying to flim-flam himself.

It reminded me of something my mother once told me. A little old lady in our town kept all her money in the bank where Mom works. A man called the lady and said he was a detective and warned her that the bank president was a suspected crook and to take out all her money and put it into another bank to be safe. She took all her life's savings out of the bank in a little sack, and the man who'd called her said he'd like to come by to make sure the money was not counterfeit before she deposited it in another bank.

While he was looking over the money in her living room, he asked her if she'd make him a cup of tea. When she came back from the kitchen with the kettle and milk pitcher, he told her he'd checked the money and the bills were all in order. He drank his tea quickly, thanked her, and left.

When the poor old lady tried to put the money in another bank, she discovered she had been flim-flammed. He had replaced all the bills with fakes and she had no money left at all!

Flim-flamming: Another word for deceiving. "Richard," I said, "if you always stick to the exact truth, nobody can ever call *you* Flim-flam."

Richard really looked mad now. "Listen, Carolyn Frankfurter, why don't you just get on your bike and pedal down to church where you belong? You're obviously going to be a creaky Sunday school teacher when you grow up, so you might as well get some praying in now that you have the free time," he said, and he stomped out of the kitchen.

TEN

My mother came home early from work the next day carrying a bag of groceries. She went straight to the kitchen and put a ham in the oven so that we'd have a nice dinner in case Richard's father decided to stay.

Then she went up to take a shower and put on her black and white dress and her new sandals. She told me to change my T-shirt when she saw the ketchup stain I'd gotten on it at lunch, and she asked me when I'd last brushed my teeth. Richard, who was still mad at me, said, "Thanksgiving."

He did not have to be told to change his shirt. He looked superclean and had changed from his beat-up old sneakers to his new moccasins. He was even wearing socks, and if they were full of holes like most of his socks, they weren't showing.

At three-fifteen he went into the living room and sat square in the middle of the couch with a copy of *Ski* magazine that had been lying around since February. When I went in there and sat on the footstool in front of the fireplace he asked me why, if there were seven rooms in the house, we both had to be in the same one. I said that this was the living room and I felt like living. He said that he felt like living too, but that being in the same room with me was not living. He got up with his magazine under his arm and marched out to the porch.

I heard him flipping the dials of the old TV set we keep out there, the one that gets only gray and white zigzags and staticky sound. A few minutes later I heard him shut it off. He came back into the living room and peered at the mantel clock and said, "What's wrong with this clock? It says three-thirty," and I said, "It *is* three-thirty," and Richard said, "I thought it was later than that."

Then he went back out to the porch. I picked up an old copy of *Dental World* and examined twelve photographs of water drills. Then Richard was back to look at the clock. "This clock is slow," he said, and he ran upstairs and reappeared with his portable radio and another old copy of *Ski*. He took those out to the porch and a minute later I heard his station blare out like he was trying to see how far in the hemisphere sound could travel.

My mother came zooming out of the kitchen. "Please turn it down, Richard. The Covellis!"

"They're still out of town," I reminded her.

"Oh, that's right. When are they due home?"

"Sunday night," I answered immediately. I was already planning on the stuff I would buy with the money I'd get then—little star earrings like Cookie's, and a new record, and a paperback called *Death of a Rock Star*.

"Still, please turn it down," she said. Richard turned it down. Mom shook her head and said in a lower voice, "When his father comes, I'll introduce you and then I think it would be best for us both to disappear, okay? They may want to have a bit of privacy."

I said okay. If I lie flat on the floor of my room and put my ear to the heat register, I can usually hear what people on the screened porch are saying.

My mother and I sat at the kitchen table eating frozen raspberry yogurt. Frozen yogurt's not bad, though nothing beats Heavenly Hash. She invited Richard to join us, but he said he wasn't hungry. While Mom was scooping out a second dish for me, we heard the temperature announced on Richard's station: eighty-four degrees. And the time: four o'clock. I saw my mother look up at the clock and then at her watch.

Richard's station began playing Golden Oldies: "The YMCA," "I Love the Night Life," "Movin' Out," and one of my favorites, "Just the Way You Are." Someone called in a request for "Tomorrow." That song always reminds me of the time I locked myself into the bathroom by mistake. It was before we had the new lock put in—when we had the old rusty one that kept jamming, and I thought I was alone in the house and that I'd be stuck up there until who-knows-when. I was a little kid then, and I imagined terrible things—like starving to death next to the sink. I started to scream, hoping someone would hear me. Richard came running, and to calm me down he brought out his cassette player and put on his tape of "Tomorrow" to be funny, but through the door he said, "I'll have you out of there before the record's finished." Although he didn't quite make it before the end of the tape, he did get me out.

I went out to the porch to listen. Richard was sitting on the rattan chaise, feet up, eyes closed. "Remember this song?" I asked.

"Sshhh," he said.

When the song was over, the announcer began talking about a new medication called X-48, guaranteed to clear up teenage blemishes within forty-eight hours. Then he played two more Golden Oldies, and finally he said, "The temperature is eighty-nine degrees, at four-thirty."

"Your father is late," I said.

Richard said, "You're in the same room as me again. And you're wearing another one of my T-shirts. How come?"

I said, "This isn't me, it's my clone," and he picked up the *Ski* magazine as if he was going to throw it at me. I left and went up to my room and looked out of the window. I could see to the corner and, yes, a car was just turning up our street. Not a Porsche, not blue, but a gray sports car with a dark red racing stripe. Was that the sort of car Richard's father might arrive in? No, it was Mr. Mackey, pulling into his driveway three houses up from ours. I watched him get out and walk across his lawn, and I watched his dog come bounding out from the backyard to greet him, and then another car turned the corner. This time it was a little yellow station wagon—certainly a car that Richard's father might drive. But it didn't stop. Neither did the convertible, the dented Volks, the elegant Seville, the blue Ford truck. Then a Porsche turned the corner! Not blue, brown. Still . . . Unfortunately, although it really looked as if it might be slowing down, it didn't. It went right by.

At five o'clock Richard's father still hadn't arrived. I went downstairs; the whole house smelled of delicious ham. My mother was standing in the door of the screened porch. "Might be the traffic, could be very heavy," she was saying. Richard didn't answer. "He might have been delayed for any number of reasons. I'll go make some biscuits, and by the time I'm finished, I'll bet he's here," she said. But when she came back, with flour on both her elbows and a little stripe of it on her forehead, Richard's father had still not arrived.

When my father came home much later, we ate the

biscuits, the ham, and corn on the cob, and by the time we'd finished our lemon ice dessert, we all knew it: Richard's father wasn't coming at all.

That night—and it must have been pretty late because I was half asleep and the house was very quiet—I heard Mom's voice coming from Richard's room.

"When I was a girl," she said, "my mother put me in a ballet class because I was a little awkward and she thought it would teach me to be lithe and to move with grace. For two or three years I practiced the *entrechat*, the *saut de basque*, and the *arabesque*. But although I was able to learn the steps and knew where to put my arms and how to hold my head, I never was really comfortable dancing, or graceful. I never learned to move like a real ballerina. I guess I just didn't have the talent. I tried to get out of ballet class whenever I could. In a way, I think it's like that with your father. Although he may have made an effort, he doesn't have the real talent it takes to be a good father. And because he's never liked doing what he's not good at, I think that, without realizing it, he tries to get out of it. He was always like that, Richard. Try not to let it hurt so much."

I didn't hear any reply from Richard, and a few minutes later I heard Mom's footsteps going toward her bedroom. After that, there was silence. I guess I fell asleep, because I remember dreaming that a blue Porsche did pull up in front of our house and Richard's father stepped out and gave Richard a big fatherly hug and then went to the trunk and opened it and there were four presents, one for each of us—four beautiful gifts wrapped in paper in every color of the rainbow.

Later that night, I woke up and thought I saw Richard in

my room, poking around near my desk, and I sat right up and said, "What are you *doing*?" and he said, "I just remembered to return the screwdriver. Shut up and go back to sleep!" I was too groggy to argue, but the next morning I jumped out of bed, looked under my clock, and there were all my keys, exactly as I'd left them, so I figured I'd dreamed that, too.

ELEVEN

Mr. and Mrs. Covelli said that their vacation was the best they'd ever had. They said the Cape was lovelier than ever and it only rained once the whole time they were there. They thanked me for taking care of Aunt Agnes, gave me fourteen single dollar bills, and said that even though their vacation had been perfect, they were really happy to be home. They said Aunt Agnes was purring like crazy and looked as if she'd really been well taken care of, the house looked fine, and wasn't that a new picnic set in our backyard? I told them how Dad had put it together with the help of their own screwdriver, and said I hoped they didn't mind our borrowing it. Mr. Covelli said of course he didn't mind and to feel free to come back and borrow it again any time. I returned their key.

That was Sunday night. On Monday, three unexpected things happened.

In the morning, a postcard came from Richard's father. On one side was a picture of the Holiday Inn in Wilmington, Delaware, and on the other side was a message. I knew I was taking my life in my hands by reading it, but a postcard is a postcard and can't be very private, can it? Not with me around, it can't.

"Dear Rickie," it said. "Sorry I couldn't make it Thursday. I got held up at a conference here in Delaware. Will try to swing up your way on my next trip. See ya, Dad."

I raced up to Richard's room with it. For the last three days he'd slept until one o'clock. Now it was only eleven, but I thought a postcard from his father was important enough a reason to wake him. He groaned and moaned when I went into his room, but finally my waving the card under his nose did it: He sat up in bed and squinted at it. I watched his face while he read, but there was no change in his eyes, nose, or mouth. He turned over the card and stared blankly at the picture of the Holiday Inn. He sort of looked as if he was reading a French restaurant menu—as if it was another language and nothing was registering. Then, letting the card fall on the floor next to his bed, he flopped back into his pillow.

"What are you going to do?" I asked. I don't know what I expected, but I guess I expected something dramatic. I thought maybe he'd tear up the card and scatter the pieces in the air like confetti, or set fire to it and watch it burn until it was a bunch of ashes. At least he could have flung it into his wastepaper basket. Actually, I was disappointed.

"Aren't you going to do anything?" I asked again.

"Yeah, I'm going to sleep," Richard said, and he rolled over and pulled the covers up over his ears.

That night, after dinner, it was my turn to empty the garbage. That's when the second unexpected thing happened. I carried the bag down to the garbage pail, and when I lifted the lid—wow!—there it was: the kite that had been tacked up over Richard's bed ever since I could remember. It was broken into bits and squashed way down in the pail. I wanted to run right back inside and tell Richard that I understood how he felt, but I just didn't know how to say it.

The third surprise came at nine-thirty, in the middle of a rerun of a Carol Burnett special we were all watching (all except Richard, who was out with Flim-flam). The telephone rang. My father went to answer it, and a few minutes later he came into the den. "It's Mrs. Covelli. For you, Carolyn."

Mrs. Covelli's voice sounded strange—not like the way it sounded when she came home from Cape Cod at all.

"Carolyn, Mr. Covelli's aunt came to dinner tonight, and when I went to the sideboard in the dining room to take out the coffeepot, I realized the silver cream pitcher is missing. I know it was here before I left, because I polished all the silver the week before our vacation. Now, I know you wouldn't borrow it like the screwdriver, dear, but is there the slightest possibility you saw it somewhere in the house? Possibly I misplaced it, stuck it into some crazy place without thinking . . . ?"

I could hardly swallow. "I didn't see it." Was that really my voice coming out of my head?

"I just can't understand it," she went on. "I'm sure I put it back right next to the sugar bowl. I'm a bit upset, not only because the silver creamer is valuable, but because it belonged to my great-grandmother. It's well over a hundred years old. So you didn't see it?"

"No, I'm sorry, I didn't."

"Well, I'll have to go through the house with a fine-tooth comb. Maybe it's just stuck in some corner behind something. I'll do that first thing tomorrow."

I said okay, tried to think of a good prayer that would really work—*Dear God, please let her find her silver pitcher, amen*—and was about to hang up when Mrs. Covelli said, "Carolyn, I was wondering . . ." My heart was going *bam/bam, bam/bam.* "You had the key the whole time, didn't you?" she asked. She sounded as if she hadn't really wanted to ask me that question at all, and it was a sure thing I didn't want her to ask me. It was also a sure thing I didn't want to answer it. But I did.

"Yes, I did," I said. My heart was going *bam/bam, bam/bam, bam/bam/bam.* What else could I say?

"All right. I'm sure I'll find the creamer sooner or later. Don't worry about it, dear. And thanks again."

Bambambambambam.

"What did she want?" my father asked when I pulled myself together and went back into the den. Carol Burnett was wearing a cleaning lady's outfit and a dustmop wig. Red.

"Nothing much," I said.

"Nothing much? She must have called for a reason."

"Something about Aunt Agnes. Nothing much," I said, and I ran into the bathroom so they wouldn't ask me anything else.

When the bambams in my chest had died down and I thought I was safe from more questions, I went up to my brother's room, pushed open the door, and turned on the light. He was still out; he'd hardly been home at all since Thursday. I'd seen Mom give Dad a look when he and Flim left, but my mother never said a thing. She didn't even ask where they were going. You couldn't talk to Richard these days anyhow; he'd just say "Yes" or "No" or "I'm busy" when you tried to have a conversation with him. And during lunch or dinner, he'd just sit there so quietly you'd think he was watching a movie on the tablecloth.

It was clear now that seeing Richard in my room in the middle of the night had been no dream. He'd taken the key, gone back to the Covellis', and probably stolen their creamer.

I zeroed in under his bed. Nothing. Then I went to his closet, poked around in the back among his old hockey sticks and ski poles. More nothing. I looked under his desk and in his desk and bureau drawers and was starting to go to work on his night table when I heard him come in the back door. He and Flim were headed up here, and if he caught me, it was a sure thing he'd do to me what he did to the old kite.

I flew out of his room and headed for the bathroom, locked the door, threw open the medicine cabinet to listen, and waited. My luck, Flim-flam needed to use the bathroom. "Come on out," Richard called. "What are you doing in there, painting a mural?"

"Use the downstairs bathroom," I said.

Flim-flam called sweetly through the door, "Come on out! I've got a ring for you, Carrie! I'll give it to you as soon as you come out!"

A ring? Had he stolen a ring now? I'd throw it right back at him! No, I'd take it right to the police this time. It wouldn't surprise me if it was a diamond or an emerald ring. Maybe a ruby. Nothing would surprise me. I opened the door.

Flim-flam grabbed me before I even got a foot out of the bathroom. He put both hands around my neck and squeezed. "Here's your wring! A *neck* wring!" he said, and he and Richard laughed as if they'd never heard anything funnier in their whole lives. Then Richard said, "Okay, Flim, that's enough," and Flim-flam let go of my neck.

"Not funny," I said.

"Oh, take it easy. He flim-flams everybody."

I looked my brother right in the eye. "Wait till he flim-flams you!" I said.

Much later, after Flim had left and Mom and Dad had gone to bed, I told my brother about Mrs. Covelli's call.

"Did you take her creamer?" I asked Richard. I was sort of whispering so I wouldn't wake Mom and Dad. We were standing in the upstairs hall. Richard had just taken a shower and was standing there dripping wet in his terry robe.

"You *are* creaky," he said. This time I couldn't look him right in the eye because he turned away fast and went into his room. I watched him make wet footprints on the hall floor.

"You did!" I whispered to the closed door. "I know you did!" I stood there in the hall for the longest time, watching the wet footsteps dry up and disappear, and not knowing what to do.

I hardly slept that night. Sometime before morning I decided I had to tell my mother what I suspected. I decided I had to tell her everything.

That afternoon, as soon as Mom came in from the bank, I followed her into the kitchen. She looked tired and seemed more interested in looking through the spice cabinet than in having a conversation, but by this time I was bursting.

First I told her about the silver cream pitcher. When I'd finished, she completely surprised me by just smiling. "Mrs. Covelli has so much stuff in that house, I'm surprised she can keep track of anything, dear. I'll bet she found it about five minutes after she called. And anyway, Richard does not give tea parties." She turned back to the cabinet. "Have you seen the oregano, Carolyn? It seems to be missing."

I said I hadn't seen it. Then I told her about Mrs. Strawheim's missing five dollars and penlight.

She listened to every word, but when I was through, she just shook her head. "Those penlights only cost about three or four dollars. Mr. Adams at the bank has one. Lots of people do. Anyway, you don't really think your brother would steal from Mrs. Strawheim, do you? . . . Now, where could I have put the oregano?"

"What about the five dollars?" I asked. "And there's more!" I told her about the purple team jackets I'd found under Richard's bed, and she shook her head again, this time emphatically. "Your brother has never stolen anything in his whole life. He's a good boy. And, Carolyn, unless you have proof, don't accuse your brother of being a thief." She frowned. "Please don't even think of mentioning any of this silly nonsense to your father. We're having enough problems with Richard as it is."

I could hardly believe that my mother, who is so sensible about a lot of things, could just be turning her back on what was happening right here, in our family. And she was acting as if *I* was the one making trouble!

"I may be only twelve years old, but I know what I know!" I cried, and she just smiled and put her arms around me like I was four years old, and she said, "I'm getting a miserable headache right at the back of my head. Would you run upstairs and get me two aspirins?" and she turned around and went right back to rummaging through the spice cabinet again, saying, "I sometimes think you kids watch too many television crime shows."

As I ran upstairs, I thought about what she'd said about having enough problems already, and I thought about her headaches. By the time I was back down, I'd promised myself that, no matter what, I wasn't going to make things worse by turning into Carolyn the Informer.

How could I even think of ratting on my own brother, anyway?

TWELVE

About a week later, I was sitting on the beach, writing a letter to Jen, when Mrs. Strawheim came over to sit next to me. She unfolded her beach chair, wobbled into it, and said she was getting so big she wouldn't be surprised if the baby turned out to be quintuplets. Then she started to oil her shoulders with suntan lotion. She asked me how I was enjoying my summer vacation and said she liked my bathing suit and talked about this and that.

Finally she pulled out her needlepoint bag and began to work on the tennis racquet cover she was making. I admired all the zigs and zags and said I'd always wanted to learn how to do needlepoint. Mrs. Strawheim said that she'd be glad to teach me how to do the stitches. I told her I'd like to do a cover for my life scrapbook, and she was really interested in that, and asked me what I was pasting in it. I explained about the souvenirs I collect—matchbooks from places we've been, my best schoolwork papers, letters and postcards, even sad stuff, like the last photograph Dad took of our dog when he was starting to get sick and we knew he was going to die.

Suddenly Mrs. Strawheim turned to me and asked if anything had been missing from our locker lately. She said she was asking because our locker was so near hers, and had we heard she was missing five dollars from a little French purse she'd left in her locker next to the beach towels a few weeks ago?

I just stared down at my toes in the sand and shook my head.

She went on: My talking about photographs had reminded her that someone had broken into the locker next to hers just yesterday, the Benedicts', and stolen a two-hundred-dollar camera and all the attachments. She said she heard other things were missing—money from the Hardwicks' locker, a box of expensive cigars from the Wargas', and at least four watches from other people who had lockers in our row. Apparently someone was climbing up over the back of the lockers, probably at night, and making quite a haul.

I could barely breathe, not to mention speak. "We don't, uh, keep many valuable things in our locker," I stammered. Mrs. Strawheim didn't seem to notice that my mouth wasn't moving right. She just kept talking: about how her little ones were enjoying their swimming lessons; how nice it was here at the club; how sad it was that somebody—she hardly imagined it could be a member—was doing such awful things; how she hoped, now that Mr. Prisco had notified the police, that the thief would soon be caught.

I said I thought I'd go for a swim.

I ran into the salt water and it was bitter cold, but I hardly felt anything except the old bambambams in my chest. They seemed to be moving up and down through my whole body and right through my head. I could feel them in my ears: BAMBAM.

I couldn't spend another minute here in the water or at the

beach, I couldn't spend another minute at the club. I had to get out, jump on my bike, and find Richard. Mr. Prisco had notified the police! Handcuffs, lawyers, a judge, jail. It had to be Flim-flam, but maybe he'd roped my brother into stealing too! I pictured Richard lying on a bare mattress in a cold and dark cell, with a murderer for a roommate.

As I was drying myself, my hands flying like the wind, Mrs. Strawheim pulled something out of her needlepoint bag. "I have an extra piece of canvas here, and some blue and green wool. Wait—I even have extra needles. If you like, I can show you a few basic stitches right now, and you can practice while you sit on the beach."

She was so nice and helpful, like Mrs. Curley, my second-grade teacher. "I—I forgot an errand I have to do for my mother," I said.

"Next time, then, Carolyn?" Mrs. Strawheim asked, smiling, as always. I nodded. "Say hello to your mother," she called after me as I ran back to the locker, the sand like a hot griddle under my feet.

My mind was racing as I dressed. *Find Richard.* I'd heard him say Flim-flam was driving him to the shopping center so Richard could get new sneakers. That was two hours ago, when I was getting ready to go to the club. Would they still be there?

Warn Richard. I jumped onto my bike and pedaled away as if it was on fire. Speeding crazily through the heavy lunch-time traffic, I kept hearing Mrs. Strawheim's words in my ears: *Mr. Prisco has notified the police.* Then I started rehearsing what I would say to Richard—"Give it back, please, give it all back!"—if I could find him.

There must have been a hundred cars in the parking lot when I got there, and that wasn't counting the back parking lot, where there may have been a hundred more. The possibility of finding Flim-flam's car here among all these other cars was nearly zero. For a minute I just stood there, wet with perspiration and almost fainting from all that pedaling. The sun, smooth and warm at the club after a cooling dip, now felt like a steam-iron pressed against my shoulders, and the smell of exhaust fumes was making me dizzy.

The shopping center is filled with stores of every kind; where was I going to begin? I dragged my bike up to the bike rack in front of the supermarket and was tempted to duck in there for a dose of arctic air-conditioning, but I was sure Richard wouldn't be there, so finally I decided to head for the sporting goods store. That seemed like the most likely place for Richard to shop for his sneakers.

As I stepped into the sporting goods store, I shivered deliciously and inhaled as much cool air as I could with one breath. It cleared my head, and I went scooting up and down the aisles looking for Richard or Flim-flam. There was no sign of them. Now that I thought of it, that was no surprise. If Richard had come here first, he'd probably already have bought his sneakers and left.

Left for where? The Poster Place? He always liked browsing through poster racks, sniffing the incense packages, and checking out weird T-shirts.

No luck. I could see at a glance, even past the beaded curtain into the black back room where they sold posters that glow in the dark, that he wasn't there.

He wasn't in Louie's Frozen Yogurt shop, he wasn't in the five-and-ten, he wasn't in Paperback Alley checking out the books and magazines, either.

Maybe he'd gone to have lunch! My own stomach was suddenly sending me hunger signals—I could smell the delicious aromas from the Taco Tent as if I'd stuck my nose right over a dish of taco sauce. I rushed around the corner and checked out all the people standing on line at the counter or sitting at booths in the back, but when I couldn't find Flim-flam or Richard, I lost my appetite like that.

There was nowhere else they could possibly be—obviously not in the hosiery center or any of the ladies' shops, not in the delicatessen or at the jewelers. They must have gone home. Or gone to another shopping center. Or driven to the discount store in East Loomis. Or . . .

The record shop! Why hadn't I thought of it right off? They could spend hours just mushing around the cassettes, browsing through the albums, checking out the Top Fifty lists. If they hadn't left, I'd definitely find them at Stereorama.

Sure enough, even before I looked into Stereorama, I heard Flim-flam's voice. As soon as I walked in I spotted him talking to the man behind the counter. He'd pulled up his shoulders and was trying to look tough. "I left it right here. I know I left it right here!"

The man was shaking his head. He was a tall guy with lots of hair and a heavy beard, and the parts of his face that weren't covered with hair were red.

Flim-flam's voice was zooming up higher and higher. "It had twenty dollars in it. You think I'm kidding?"

The man was still shaking his head.

Flim's voice came flying like karate chops now. "My driver's license! The car registration, my I.D. cards, the whole bit!"

"I didn't see your wallet!" the man was saying. "I'm sorry, kid, I just didn't see it!"

But where was my brother? Flim was throwing his arms up, making such a big commotion that he didn't notice me slip in. I went to the back of the store and found Richard at the cassette counter. Just as I was about to open my mouth—to tell him I was here, to warn him about Mr. Prisco and the police—my blood froze.

My brother was slipping a cassette tape under his shirt.

I saw it in a flash, how Flim-flam was pretending to have lost his wallet, making a fuss, flim-flamming the record store clerk, keeping his attention at the front of the shop while Richard was shoplifting in the back.

My brother, the thief.

"Richard," I said, and my voice went so sick in my throat I couldn't get another word out. For no reason at all I thought about the time I'd fallen off my bike and he'd been there to help me, and I thought about the time he'd gotten me out of the bathroom when I was locked in, and I thought about the time, just a couple of weeks ago, when he'd made Flim-flam give back the French fries he'd stolen off my plate, and it was as if those two French fries had jammed in my throat; no words could come out of my mouth.

He spun around, and when I saw his face, I felt even worse. Everything got very blurry, and my throat felt like it did the time Flim-flam had both hands squeezing my neck.

My brother, really a thief.

His face looked scared and red. "Get outta here, go home! Hurry up!" he whispered.

My legs wouldn't move. I think I said "Richard" a couple of more times, and I think I managed to say, "You're going to get caught. I know you're going to get caught!" but it was all I could get out. I finally turned around so he wouldn't see my face, which probably looked as rubbery as it felt, and I left the store.

I didn't want to go home, and I didn't want to go back to the club either. So I just got back on my bike and started pedaling, and without really meaning to, I wound up in front of my mother's bank. I just stood there on the sidewalk for a long time looking in and imagining what it would be like if a man walked in with a briefcase, not with a bunch of perfume bottles inside, but with a real gun, filled with bullets. I couldn't help thinking what it would be like if he went inside and shot the tellers dead, one by one. I pictured my mother lying face down on the floor and the bank robber standing over her body, and then I imagined looking into the robber's face and seeing that it was Richard.

I guess I really have been watching too many crime shows on television, but I suppose if a kid can lift cassettes from a record shop and if he can steal stuff out of lockers, he could just as easily wind up robbing banks. And although it's not likely he's going to shoot his own mother dead, he might someday shoot someone else's.

The thought started me shaking. Here it was, nearly ninety degrees outside, the sun feeling hotter than a self-cleaning oven, and I was shaking like a leaf in November.

I wanted my mother; isn't that crazy? I wanted to run inside the bank and admit that although I was really very grown up for twelve, sometimes I did feel four, and sometimes I needed her to put her arms around me and promise me that my brother wouldn't steal another thing ever, that he wouldn't get caught, that they wouldn't take him away, that everything would be safe at home and that we'd be together like every other family always.

I started to run into the bank, but through the smoked-glass window I saw my mother behind the counter, with a long line of people waiting to see her to cash checks, to deposit money or to get change. She looked so busy and so tired that I stopped right in my tracks.

Anyway, I had promised myself never to rat, hadn't I?

So instead of running into the bank, I took a deep breath and climbed back on my bike and pedaled slowly home.

THIRTEEN

When I got to the house, Cookie was on our front step, ringing the bell.

"Hi, Carolyn. Is your brother home?" she called out as I pedaled up the driveway.

"I don't know," I said. I was still very shaky, and really in no mood for conversation.

"I just came by to return his locker key. He left it at my house last night, and I know he'll be needing it. I thought I'd give it to him at the club today, but he wasn't there."

I pushed the kick stand of my bike down and walked across the lawn to take the key for Richard. As I got closer to Cookie, I noticed something new. She was wearing sunglasses with gorgeous, shiny silver frames and big, beautiful purple lenses. "I love your new sunglasses, Cookie," I said.

"I love them, too," she said, and she blushed a little. "Richard gave them to me." Her voice went up and down.

"Ooooh. Was it your birthday?" I asked.

"No. He just wanted to give me a present, I guess. And he knows I love silver. Anything silver. Look at this!" She stuck her hand in her pocket and pulled out a little, old-fashioned silver whistle. "Isn't it beautiful?" she asked. "I'm going to get a chain and hang it around my neck."

I was getting uneasy. "It's very nice," I said.

"And you know what else he gave me?" Cookie whispered. Her voice was going more down than up this time. "A little bunch of flowers from your garden. I guess 'cause I gave him some from ours. In a silver vase. Well, it's not exactly a vase, it's an antique cream pitcher, actually. I think it used to belong to your—I mean Richard's—grandmother. Don't tell your mother, now. I'm not sure she knows he took the portulacas out of her garden. I sneezed a couple of times, but I love flowers. I'm going to press them."

Antique cream pitcher was practically all I heard. It was as if she'd screamed it in my ear.

"What's the matter with you, Carolyn? Are you all right?" Cookie wanted to know.

I shook my head.

"Shall I go inside with you? You look funny."

I shook my head faster. "I'll tell Richard you stopped by," I said, and I ran across the lawn and down the driveway, past Mrs. Covelli, who was sunning herself in her backyard, with Aunt Agnes on the grass next to her feet, and who called, "Hi, Carolyn!" to me as I flew by.

As if nothing had happened.

"Look what I brought!" my father shouted upstairs when he arrived home about an hour later. He was home early and sounded really cheerful.

I went to the top of the stairs and looked down. "Look at these!" he called up to me. He held out his hand to show me what was in it.

"Tulip bulbs. Mr. Farquar was so grateful I saved his

molar, he brought me a great big bunch. I have more in the car. All colors, Mr. Farquar said."

"Oh," I said.

"You and Richard and I can plant them after dinner, when it's cooled off a bit. I guess we've got enough here to make the place look like Holland next spring!"

"I'm really tired, Dad," I said. Right now, even if Dad had brought home magic beanstalk bulbs, I wouldn't have gone downstairs to look.

Dad's face fell. I'd never realized before how interested he was in tulips. I guess he'd never realized before how *un*interested *I* was in tulips.

"Don't you feel well, Carolyn?" he wanted to know.

"I'm okay," I said, and I went back to my room to lie on my bed and stare at the ceiling.

I was still staring at the ceiling when I heard Richard come home. I heard Dad telling him about the tulip bulbs, and I heard Richard answer, "I think I'd rather go up and take a shower and listen to music," and then I heard Dad say, "Okay." Dad didn't follow Richard upstairs or try to continue the conversation, but when Mom came home later I heard his voice downstairs and all the zing had gone out of it.

That's the way I felt, too, as if all the zing had gone out of me.

I went to Richard's door and knocked twice, and his voice came out sounding half asleep. When he finally opened the door a crack, I told him about Mr. Prisco and the police, and he said, "Stay out of it," and tried to close the door.

I whispered, "Richard, they'll catch you!" and he said, "Not if you keep your mouth closed, Carolyn Frankfurter! Now go away!" I just couldn't find the strength to keep my sneaker between the door and the frame; I let him close the door, went down to the den, and sat in front of the TV, trying to look as if nothing had happened.

After dinner, while I was rinsing the dishes and Richard was clearing the table, I heard Dad say, in his let's-get-down-to-business voice: "One more offer, Richard." Richard stopped clearing and waited politely to hear the offer, and my father said, "Why don't we get up very early tomorrow, really early, and head down to the club before anyone else comes and I'll try to show you the sidestroke? It's very easy, we'll start at the shallow end, and there'll be no one there to get in our way. How about it?"

Richard didn't answer. He just picked up the salt and pepper shakers and headed for the kitchen.

"Didn't you hear me, Rich?" Dad's voice had an edge.

"I heard you," Richard said.

I felt as if I might start shaking again.

"Then why didn't you answer?" my father asked. His voice now sounded as if it were turning sharp corners on two wheels.

Richard just stood in the doorway, squeezing the salt shaker in one fist, and the pepper shaker in the other, and then he said, "Can't—you—just—leave—me—alone!" It was as if suddenly a stiff silence had fallen all over every one of us, as if all sound had been turned off in the world.

After what seemed like ten years of silence, Mom said, "Richard, Dad is making you a very kind offer." Her voice sounded as if it were coming out of the Grand Canyon. Richard didn't answer. He just stood there, with the shakers, looking as if he might hurl them through a window or plunge them like boulders straight through the dining room floor.

But he just turned and went into the kitchen and set them on the counter next to me. His face was bright pink and covered with perspiration. For a minute I thought he looked just like Mom, but when I looked again, I could see I'd been wrong; he didn't look like her at all.

"I don't *understand* you!" my father's voice boomed from the dining room.

And my brother's voice, softer than the rush of a breeze along grass, so soft I could barely hear it, said, "I know."

As our sentence for the following day, Dad ordered us to clean out the basement, tie up old newspapers in bundles and put them at the curb for the recycling pickup, wash the tiles in the bathroom, and throw out the magazines in the attic.

As I was falling asleep that night, I whispered, "I hate you, Richard"; but even as I said it, I knew that even if he had stolen a million dollars and the crown jewels and fifty mink coats out of fifty beach lockers, I couldn't tell anyone he was stealing. And it wasn't because I was afraid he'd broadcast my middle name to the whole world. He was my brother, and I'd always love him even when I hated him. No matter what, to the rest of the world I'd always try to look as if nothing at all had happened, as if he were a kid like every other kid and we were like any other family you'd see out together on the street, or sitting side by side on the beach.

FOURTEEN

We split it up this way: I'd wash the bathroom tiles, Richard would throw out the magazines in the attic, and we'd both do the newspapers and the basement.

Actually, since it turned out to be a cool day, I didn't really mind cleaning the bathroom tiles. It even gave me a good feeling to scrub and scrub and make them clean and shiny, and the disinfectant spray I used gave the bathroom a real washed-down spring-flower smell. I finished the upstairs bathroom in no time and began work on the one downstairs, and because that only has one small tiled area around the sink and wasn't dirty at all, I was finished in record time.

"All done!" I called up the stairs to the attic, hoping Richard would come down and admire my sparkling work, but I guess he couldn't hear me—he'd brought his radio up there and it was blasting away. I heard him moving around, the floorboards were creaking, so I figured he'd be finished soon too. I sat at the bottom of the attic steps and waited.

And waited.

"What's taking you so long?" I called up a couple of times, but I guess the radio drowned out my voice again.

"How long does it take to pick up a bunch of magazines, anyway?" I screamed a few minutes later. No answer. He'd probably found another bunch of old *Ski* magazines and was sitting up there on a trunk reading or something. I decided to go up to investigate.

But when I was halfway up the stairs, Richard appeared at the top of the steps. "What do you want?" he asked.

"I finished like two days ago. What are you doing up there, anyhow?"

"Deep-sea fishing. What do you think I'm doing? I'm cleaning the attic."

"Aren't you almost done? We still have the whole basement to do."

'Yeah. I'm all done," Richard said, and he started to come downstairs with an armload of old magazines.

"Did you do a good job? Let's see," I said, and I tried to walk up another few steps to get a look, but he blocked my way.

"What's to see?" he asked. "It's all done. I piled up the magazines, and I'll have to make a few more trips and that's it."

I never would have been suspicious if he hadn't tried to stop me from looking around up there, but now it was an absolutely fixed and sure thing that there was something in the attic he didn't want me to see. "I'll come up and help you carry them down," I said, watching his face carefully.

"Forget it, not necessary," Richard said.

"No problem. I'll help," I said, but he pulled the attic door closed and practically pushed me down the stairs ahead of him.

"If you decide not to go in for preaching, you can always become a private eye, Snoopo," Richard said.

So I did something I'd never dared do before: I defied him. I took him by surprise, shoved him out of the way, and ran up past him to the attic to look. Of course, he came running up right behind me, but by that time I was already there.

There was the rack of winter clothes in one corner, the box of old Halloween costumes in the other, the textbooks Dad had used in college, an old diaper pail and high chair that I used to use, an empty hamster cage, a bunch of old toys and games with this much dust all over them, the outdated globe of the world, and the two old camp trunks we only used the one summer Richard and I were sent to tennis camp.

Nothing out of the ordinary.

Furthermore, Richard had done exactly what Dad had told him to do—tied bunches of magazines into tidy stacks, ready to be put at the curb—and not only that, he'd straightened up the other stuff, too. The place looked much neater than it had last week when I came up searching for my old bike pump. Everything seemed in perfect order.

"Finished with the inspection, Sergeant Snoopo?"

Now I felt embarrassed, as if I'd accused the President of the United States of cheating at gin rummy.

"I guess so," I said.

"Then let's go," he said, but just as he said "go," his voice went absolutely dead and he stopped stock-still in front of the little round window under the eaves. He'd seen something outside that froze him to the spot. I let my eyes follow his and saw it too.

A light blue police car with a flashing red light was parked in front of the Covellis' and a policeman was going up the walk: gray uniform, black tie, black gun in holster. I reached out for the insulation on the wall and clung to it so I wouldn't slide right to the floor.

"Will you pull your creaky self together?" Richard said. "He's probably selling tickets to the police league ballgame or something." But his smile was gone, and the twitching of his lip was a dead giveaway: He was scared, too.

We watched as the front door was opened and the policeman went into the house. The temperature up here felt like a heat wave in Equatorial Africa and the police car stayed at the curb for two light years. That's how long it seemed. Finally the policeman came out again. But instead of heading for his car, he cut across the driveway, aiming straight for our front door!

This is it, I thought. The doorbell sounded faintly from below.

"The doorbell, he's ringing our doorbell!" I breathed.

"He'll go away," Richard said. "Just wait and shut up."

I didn't believe it for a minute. On television when the policeman rings your doorbell and no one answers, he doesn't go away. He calls the station and pretty soon forty more policemen come jumping out of twenty cars with sirens and flashing lights, and then someone breaks down the door—and That's It.

"I'm dying," I said.

"If only," my brother whispered. His shirt was all wet and sticking to his back and under his arms.

And then the policeman just turned around and left. He walked calmly down our walk like any ordinary person, walked to his car, got in, and a minute later drove off. No sirens, no reinforcements, no nothing.

Richard smiled ear to ear. "See?" he said. "I told ya. It was nothing."

I was so relieved I wanted to throw my arms around him and hug him.

I almost did it, too, but when I turned around, my eye suddenly caught a glint of light in the corner.

My brother's camp trunk had a brand-new lock, shining bright gold in the dim glow of the attic bulb. Shining like an evil idol's eye in a dark temple.

How could I have missed it?

FIFTEEN

"It's all the stolen stuff, isn't it?" I asked Richard.

"Let's get moving and do the basement," he said, and started down the attic stairs.

"All of it. Up here in the attic. And the policeman was ringing our doorbell two minutes ago." I looked at the shining lock and shuddered.

"Are you coming down, Snoopo?" Richard called. I'd obviously been talking to myself.

"Dad's going to find it sooner or later, don't think he's not!" I yelled. "And he's going to call the police. They'll come back. And they're going to take you away!"

"Will you get yourself down here before I stuff you into that hamster cage?"

I followed Richard to the basement and picked up a broom. While I moved across the floor, sweeping like a battery-operated robot, Richard started tying up the newspapers that Mom had put in piles near the door to the garage.

We hadn't been down there five minutes when the doorbell rang again. I grabbed the broom handle and spun around to look at Richard; he spun around to look at me. We must have had the same thought: The police were back!

"Not a word about the trunk," Richard said under his breath.

I nodded. I couldn't have talked if they'd tortured me with water drips. Richard went upstairs while I held on to my broom for dear life. A minute later I heard the front door slam and then loud laughter—Flim-flam's. For once I was happy to hear his voice.

"Hello, Carrie," he said, plopped himself on a pile of newspapers, and smiled at me like he'd just been named Charming Kid of the Year. I was too nervous to answer.

He pulled a stuffed brown sock out of his pocket. "I got the you-know-what," he said to Richard, winking.

Richard sent me upstairs for a glass of lemonade with "lots of ice," to get me out of there, and Flim-flam said he'd help me by sweeping up if I wanted to take a little rest and to take my time "squeezing the lemons." Whatever was in the sock was "it"—probably one more stolen something I wasn't supposed to know about. I played along, saying I'd take a rest and be down as soon as the frozen lemonade had defrosted. Actually I headed straight for the heat register in the dinette. If I kneel next to it, I can hear pretty much what's being said in the basement.

I knelt down and listened. . . . They were fighting! "Get that sock out of here!" Richard was saying.

"Are you kidding? You know what this stuff is worth?"

"I don't care. Get it out of here!"

"Keep cool, Rich! Does your old lady have any little plastic bags laying around?"

"I told ya—" Richard's voice was so loud that I had to draw back from the register.

"What's the big deal? I mix it with a whole bunch of oregano, we make up a million nickel bags and sell them for five dollars each, and we're rich. Nobody can tell the difference. I made two hundred bucks before school closed. Easy!"

Oregano! Flim-flam had been stealing it from my mother to mix with the pot he was selling. Selling dope and flim-flamming at the same time; nice kid.

"I can't fool around with that. And I don't want it in the house."

Good for you, Rich, I thought. *Now throw him out!*

"Come on, get down, will ya, Rich? What do you think is gonna happen if they catch you?"

I didn't hear Richard's answer to that, although I really would have liked to; it's all I'd been thinking of the whole summer.

"Nothing's gonna happen! First time you go to family court, you stand there looking really straight. Pathetic. You wear a suit and a tie, your lawyer says you're really a wonderful kid and tells the judge how you've been going to church every Sunday all your life. The judge sits there in his black nightgown and asks if you've been going to school regularly, and your lawyer says, 'Absolutely,' and your mother stands there with a tear in each blue eye and the judge says, 'I'll give him an Adjournment in Contemplation of Dismissal,' which means you go home free as a bird."

I held my breath. *Don't listen, Richard.*

"I want the pot out of here and the stuff out of the attic, too!" Richard said, practically shouting. I wanted to give him a round of applause. "I told ya I don't want any of it in my house!"

"Listen, we're gonna sell it, aren't we? I told you the friend of a friend who's gonna buy it is on vacation. Didn't I say he'd be back on Labor Day?"

"I changed my mind. You can do whatever you want—just leave me out of it!"

"Hey, what are you so nervous about, Mother?"

I had my ear very close to the heat register, so I know I heard the answer right. Richard said: "My sister."

Me?

Flim-flam's laugh came up sounding like the canned laughs in TV movies—short and fake. "Your *sister*? You gotta be kidding! Are you gonna try to protect that little nerd from the wicked, evil world?"

"Shut up," Richard said. "Just shut up."

When Dad came home, he went first to check out the basement, and he said we'd done a good job. Then he examined the bathrooms I'd scrubbed. "Perfect," he said. "Carolyn, you really made those tiles gleam." He squeezed two singles into my hand and kissed the top of my head. Then he said to both of us, "Come on, let's have a look at the attic."

My heart was in my mouth; all I could see was the old trunk with its new lock. I imagined it winking and blinking at us through the dim light like the yellow caution light at the school corner. I kept glancing at Richard and he looked uneasy, too—silent and unsteady.

But when we got to the attic, Dad saw something else. He saw the attic straightened up and clean for the first time in ages. He saw the way Richard had followed his orders to the letter, carried through exactly the way he'd been told. All smiles and compliments, Dad grasped Richard's shoulder and said he was really proud of him for a job well done. He slipped Richard a few bills, too, and then turned and started downstairs. He'd never even looked at the trunk!

I stole a quick look at Richard, and although I expected to see him smiling and pleased, he wasn't smiling at all. In fact, he looked miserable.

I saw something else. Lying next to Richard on the floor was something flat and round, gleaming like glass.

"What's that?" I asked. Maybe some other valuable stolen thing had dropped out of the trunk or Richard's pocket.

He looked down, scooped it up quickly, and put it behind his back. "Nothing. Let's break camp," Richard said, and in a way I guess I really didn't want to know. I didn't argue, just turned and left the attic without another word.

An hour later, almost as soon as Mom came home, she and Dad left to go to a cookout.

Although I was in no mood, Mom had put me in charge of making tuna salad and hard-boiled eggs for Richard's and my dinner, and I was too busy in the kitchen to realize that Richard was still up there in the attic, alone. When I'd put the salad on the table and called him three times and he didn't answer, I went looking for him.

He was sitting on the trunk, in the half-dark. The one dim bulb hanging under the eaves was throwing big, spooky shadows all over the walls.

Richard was just sitting there, in front of his own monster shadow, staring at the floor.

"Didn't you hear me call you?" I asked.

No answer.

"Dinner is ready." No answer.

I waited.

"I'm not hungry," Richard finally said.

"I heard you fighting with Flim-flam," I said.

"It figures. You got ears all over your head."

"I don't get it. If you don't want the stuff, why'd you steal it?"

"M.Y.O.B.," Richard said.

"It just doesn't make sense!"

Richard suddenly put both hands up to his face and bent over, and I got so scared I felt as if all the blood was rushing out of my head and into my neck and body. Then he started to shake.

It was the first time I could remember that I'd seen Richard cry and it was a sound worse than anything I'd ever heard; it seemed to ricochet off the floor and walls and go right through my skin and into my heart.

Finally he stopped and wiped his eyes with the palms of his hands and he said, "Why did I steal all that stuff?" He looked at me but didn't really seem to see me at all. "Because I'm no good," he whispered. "Because I'm just like my father."

SIXTEEN

The policeman came back Saturday morning, just as Dad was putting wheat germ on his cereal. We were planning to all go to the club to have a picnic on the beach. Richard was still sleeping, and I was having orange juice and trying to remember where I'd left the open can of tennis balls I'd used last week. Then the doorbell rang.

After what happened yesterday, I should have been prepared for what came next, but I wasn't. Maybe it was too early and I was still half asleep, but when I got to the door and saw the policeman with his uniform and badge and behind him the police car at the curb, the floor seemed to seesaw right under my feet.

"Are you Carolyn Desmond?" the policeman asked me.

The floor was definitely moving. In fact, so was the whole room. I nodded.

"Are your parents in?" he asked.

It wasn't necessary to answer that, because my father had appeared in the living room doorway and my mother had appeared on the stairs, and they both simultaneously asked,

"Who is it?" Then, spotting the policeman, my father said, "Can I help you?" and my mother said, "Is anything wrong?" and the policeman said he was Patrolman Quinn and asked if he could come in for a moment; he had some questions he wanted to ask me.

Me?

The room was really spinning now, taking off, like a ride at the amusement park. Patrolman Quinn stepped into the room and somehow I backed into the fireplace. I grabbed onto it to steady myself, but it wasn't helping much. I caught sight of my face reflected in one of my father's loving cup tennis trophies on the mantel, and even the reflection seemed to be swaying. I kept thinking of the attic, the trunk, the terrible shining-eye lock, the stolen stuff inside—cameras and watches and money and who knows what else.

"I'm sorry to bother you," Patrolman Quinn said. He took off his sunglasses and I saw a pair of very light eyes under a pair of very dark eyebrows. I felt as if two searchlights were throwing beams at me.

"No bother at all," said my father, who had come into the room and was now standing next to me. I held tight to the fireplace.

My mother was halfway between the stairs and the coffee table; she was wearing a flowered housecoat with a bow tie around the neck, and one of her hands was playing with the knot of the tie.

"Mrs. Covelli has reported some things missing from her house and she's putting in an insurance claim. This is a routine inquiry we have to make, since she said Carolyn was in possession of her key while she and her husband were in . . ." Patrolman Quinn took a piece of paper out of his pocket and read, "Cape Cod?" as if it were a question.

Things were missing? Was one cream pitcher "things"?

"That's right, Officer, go ahead," Mom said.

"Thank you," he said. "Now, Carolyn." He turned to me and I felt my fingers pressing hard against the brick of the fireplace. "When you were holding the key to Mrs. Covelli's house, where did you keep it?"

"In my room," I said. I surprised myself by sounding almost like a normal person.

"Where in your room did you keep it?" the policeman went on.

"In an envelope. On my dresser. Under my digital clock."

"I hope Mrs. Covelli isn't accusing Carolyn of taking her silly cream pitcher," my mother said. She sounded irritated and nervous at the same time.

"No, no, not at all," Patrolman Quinn said. "It's just something we have to follow up. And it involves more than a cream pitcher."

The room almost turned upside down. More than a cream pitcher?

Patrolman Quinn checked his papers again. "The Covellis are also missing forty-five dollars in cash and an antique police whistle. They discovered that loss a few days ago. It's an heirloom, I guess. Mrs. Covelli's grandfather was a police constable in England, and the whistle was his. It's over a hundred years old."

Richard's gift to Cookie! I wished the room would really spin away and take us all with it. *Oh, Richard!*

"Carolyn, you don't know anything about this, do you?" my father asked. He'd come up very close to me and had his hand on my arm.

I just shook my head. I wanted to say no, but the word was jammed down there in my throat and wouldn't come out.

Dad put his arm around my shoulder. "My daughter would never—" He never got to say "steal."

"Don't worry, Dr. Desmond," Patrolman Quinn interrupted. "This is not in any way an accusation against your daughter. As I said, it's a routine inquiry. Mrs. Covelli made it very clear that she's known your family for many years and never had any suspicion that Carolyn could be involved. She just wondered if somehow the key could have fallen into the wrong hands. Now, I understand you also have a son . . ."

Dad looked annoyed. "Our son wouldn't steal either," he and Mom said together, almost like a chorus. They looked at each other. My mother was twisting the tie at her throat, turning it in this and that direction; I couldn't take my eyes from her moving fingers. For a second, she looked at me. I guess she remembered what I'd told her, but I knew she still didn't believe it.

"Don't misunderstand. I'm not here to accuse your son either. I would like to talk to you about his friend, John Sullivan, though. We've had him under periodic surveillance and know he's been spending some time over here."

"John Sullivan?" My mother looked blank.

"Flim-flam," I reminded her.

"Carolyn, go and wake Richard," Dad said. "He should be in on this."

As it turned out, it wasn't necessary to wake Richard. I found him standing in his robe and slippers at the top of the stairs, where he'd been listening quietly, taking it all in, just the way I do when I press my ear to the heat registers or the medicine cabinet. He followed me downstairs and Dad introduced him to Patrolman Quinn, and they actually calmly shook hands. All the time, I was watching Richard's face, seeing it tense and polite the way it was now, but remembering the way it looked when I saw him sitting on the trunk in the attic under the lightbulb when it was all wet and streaked with tears.

He told Patrolman Quinn he didn't know anything about the key to the Covellis'. He said he'd never gone into the house except to borrow a screwdriver, and he kept a straight face the whole time—straight, that is, except for his lower lip, which was twitching. I saw it; hadn't my parents noticed? I looked first at my father, who seemed as stiff and unmoving as one of the trees in our front yard, and my mother, whose fingers were still traveling up and down her bow tie. Her eyes were going from Richard's face to Patrolman Quinn's to Dad's.

"Now what's all this about the Sullivan kid?" Dad wanted to know.

Then Patrolman Quinn began to tell us about "John Sullivan." He said Flim's father was dead and his mother—Patrolman Quinn stopped and looked at me, probably wondering whether he should say this in front of me—was "not a very good mother." She had too many boyfriends, is what he meant. The one now living at the Sullivan house—Bill—drank a lot, had no job, and had a police record.

Film-flam had been in trouble many times, too, and Patrolman Quinn recited a few of Flim's previous crimes: truancy, shoplifting (I got hot and cold when Patrolman Quinn said "shoplifting"), and possession of a concealed weapon (I got even hotter and colder when he said possession of a weapon). I remembered seeing something like a knife in the glove compartment of his car, remembered the way the long, sharp blade gleamed.

Mom looked at Dad, and Dad looked at Mom. Patrolman Quinn said that Flim-flam was a PINS, which, he explained, stands for Person In Need of Supervision. He was to report to a youth officer every two weeks. Patrolman Quinn said that since Flim-flam turned sixteen, his status as youthful offender had changed; if he was caught committing a crime now, he could be sent to a penitentiary.

"Penitentiary" is a word that gives me the tremors. It makes me think of people trapped all their lives in little iron-barred cells, people sleeping on narrow mattresses crawling with cockroaches.

In two months Richard was going to turn sixteen, too.

My mother was staring at me. She had seen my face, probably noticed *my* lower lip trembling. No wonder Richard had told Flim-flam he had to have the stuff out of the house because of me. Even if I never said anything, my face and body weren't good at keeping secrets.

Mom threw me a pull-yourself-together look, and then she said, "I'm afraid some of this may be upsetting my daughter, Officer." He apologized, and she nodded and said she thought she'd better take me upstairs.

Patrolman Quinn apologized again and said he would leave right away, but he wanted to ask me one last question. Was it possible that Flim-flam had somehow gotten hold of Mrs. Covelli's key? I swallowed hard and said I didn't think so.

Officer Quinn jotted something down in his notebook. Then he thanked us politely and left.

Almost the minute the door had closed behind the policeman, Mom and Dad turned to Richard and fired question marks at him with their eyes. Richard had been inching out of the living room into the hall and was starting to walk upstairs. He said, "I don't know anything about it," but he turned his face away, so we couldn't see it. Then Dad said, "Are you sure?" and Richard said, "I'm sure," over his shoulder and kept climbing the stairs. Dad called him back. "Come back here a minute, please, Rich," he said, and Richard said, "I can't, I have a date."

Dad said, "Come back anyway, I want to say something before you leave."

Richard stopped on the stairs and turned around, but he didn't come down. Dad said, "I don't want you hanging around with that Sullivan kid. We had no idea about his police record."

Richard just stood on the steps staring down at my father, not answering.

"Did you hear what I said?" Dad's face was dark and cloudy.

Richard nodded.

"Then I'd like you to promise to keep as far away from him as possible."

Mom went to the foot of the stairs. "You heard what the policeman said about him, Richard," she said.

"I don't think he's that bad. Anyway he's been a good buddy," Richard said. I didn't like the hard look I saw creeping into his eyes.

"He's not the kind of buddy we'd like for you," Dad said.

Richard tilted his head to the side the way tough crooks do on TV when they're about to kick a gun out of someone's hand. "Why not?" he asked. Even his voice had a new something in it, a sort of hard wham.

"Because it sounds to me as if he's just no good," Dad said.

There was a pause and then Richard said, "Like me." His voice was so quiet, I hardly heard it.

Mom said, "That's ridiculous!" and then she asked it as if it were a question someone from an invisible audience was going to step in to answer: "Isn't that ridiculous?" and Dad answered, "Yes, it's ridiculous," and although he hadn't changed his position or raised his voice, I could feel his fury crackling from the living room to the hall, up the stairs and back again.

Then Dad said, "I forbid you to see that boy again, Richard."

Richard didn't move. He just kept his head tilted to the side and held tight to the bannister, and he said, "You can't forbid me to do anything."

"What does that mean?" Dad demanded, and the hurricane was up; I felt it coming. Richard's voice snapped like the mast of a ship in a high wind. "I mean that you're not my father, so don't tell me what to do!"

"Not my father" hung in the air.

"Richard!" my mother cried. Her head jerked toward my father, who was taking huge, striding steps toward Richard.

"You're not going to order me around!" Richard cried.

My father had his arm raised, was leaping up the steps, was actually going to . . . *beat*? *smash*? . . . Richard.

I nearly stopped breathing.

"Don!" my mother cried. Dad froze, stood there on the third step, let his arm fall to his side. It was as if the film had snapped in the middle of a movie. Finally he said, "I'm sorry, Richard. Hitting you is not the answer," and he turned and walked slowly back down the steps.

Richard's eyes were rimmed with bright red. "You see! You couldn't even let go enough to take a punch at me! Mister Self-Control! Mister Perfect! I mean, *Doctor* Perfect! Always doing everything right! Well, I'm not like you, can you see that? I'm not a bit like you! I don't like hard work. I'm not going to work my way through dental school! I'm not going to be great, super, excellent, wonderful, like you! Don't expect any trophies from me! I'm like my *real* father. *Just like him!*"

SEVENTEEN

After that scene, Richard ran up to his room, slammed the door so hard the house practically shook, stormed around behind his closed door for about ten minutes, and then went out without a word. From the window I saw him, in a blue shirt and jeans, run out the back door, jump on his bike, and pedal away, almost flying down the street.

Mom and Dad and I went to the beach as if nothing had happened—and yet as if everything had happened. We hardly spoke at all except to say polite things to each other in the car and sitting in our beach chairs. Dad and I swam for a while, but we didn't race the way we usually do, and Mom didn't want my help doing the crossword puzzle, didn't want to play rummy, didn't want to watch me do a dive from the high board. She said she had a headache at the back of her head. I opened the lunch basket, but we all just picked at our food. Dad said he guessed he wasn't much in the mood for a picnic after all.

When I was having a soft pretzel at the Deck later, Cookie

came by and said she had run into Richard, who told her he was going for a long bike ride and that he wanted to be alone. "Is something wrong?" she wanted to know, and I started to get a headache of my own, at the front of my head. I was worried that he might have run away and that I wouldn't see him at all for who knows how long. I went back to where Mom and Dad were sitting, and although it wasn't even five o'clock, I was glad when they suggested we go back home.

There was no sign of my brother when we got there, either. His bike wasn't in the garage and there were no crumbs or empty glasses in the sink, no sign he'd been home for lunch. Mom put out cold chicken for dinner, and he didn't show up when we were eating, nor afterwards, when we were cleaning up.

Dad had gone upstairs to take a shower while Mom and I were putting the leftovers in the refrigerator. I asked her what would happen if Richard didn't come back.

"He'll come back," Mom said, but she didn't sound too sure. She looked tired, and I'd just seen her reach for the aspirin bottle, even though she'd already taken a couple about an hour before.

"Why is he acting like that?" I asked. I wanted her to sit down with me and promise me Richard would be back, that he and Dad would make up and be friends again. I wanted her to explain why Richard would suddenly act crazy, scream, cry, slam doors, run away. Steal.

"I think it's partially his age. Sometimes when you're a teenager, things seem to turn upside down. What's more important is that he hates himself. When you hate yourself, it's hard to love anyone else."

"Why does he hate himself?" I asked.

My mother sat down, leaning her head in her hand. "I'm

not sure," she said. Then she looked up at me. "He can't seem to talk to me. And he can't seem to talk to your father. Maybe you can reach him, Carolyn."

Me? Every time he saw me Richard told me to M.Y.O.B or get out of his room. Every time I tried to ask him anything, he brushed me off. How was *I* going to get through to him?

"Impossible," I said, and my headache began to move from the front of my head to the back of my head. "I have a headache just like yours," I told Mom.

She sort of smiled. "Isn't it awful," she said, "that loving someone can actually give you a pain that moves from your heart into your head?" She told me to go lie down and take a rest.

Instead of lying down in my own room, I went into Richard's. I told myself it was because it was cooler there and that his bed was more comfortable, but I don't think that's the reason. I guess I wanted to be sure that when he came home I'd know it.

I took off my shoes, let them drop on the floor next to the bed, and stretched out. I looked at the place on the wall where the kite had been; two little nails it had hung from were still sticking out, and somehow it made the rest of the wall look vacant. Maybe for his birthday I could buy him a poster to put up, anything to cover that big, empty space. If he came back.

Empty spaces: I started to think about the big empty space Richard would leave in our house if he never came home. It's funny, but I guess Richard's room was just not meant for twelve-year-old eyes, because I looked around and, believe it or not, my eyes wet up with baby tears just looking at all his Richard-type junk that had been lying around for years.

Then, through a blur, I noticed something on his desk. It

was a cigar box he used to keep his matchbook collection in years ago. I hadn't seen that box in a million years.

I stared at it. It was taped shut with little strips of adhesive tape on three sides. That meant he didn't want anyone looking inside it. Taping it meant "Keep Out, Top Secret." I got up to take a closer look. I shook it a little. Something rattled. Could it break? Crumble? Explode? I set the box down fast.

"Maybe *you* can reach him," my mother had said. It was stupid to think that snooping into Richard's personal property was going to help me reach him. It was also stupid not to think that it might help.

I picked up the box again. If I carefully unpeeled the three strips of adhesive, I could take a fast peek and then tape it shut again. Even while a voice in my head was screaming no, no, no, my fingers were playing with the tape. One by one, the tape strips loosened. It was so easy. I lifted the lid of the box.

Ohmygosh. Inside, the thing I'd seen him hide behind his back in the attic, shiny, glass, round. A photo in an oval frame!

It was getting darker outside; I wanted a clearer look. I took the photo to the window, let the last of the twilight fall directly on it. It was my mother's wedding picture, not the one taken when she married my father, not a copy of the one she had on her bedroom dresser in the big gold frame, but this strange one. The picture taken of her in her white dress and veil when she was married to Richard's father!

I gaped at the picture for what seemed like ten minutes. I'd never seen it before—Mom in a real white wedding dress so long that a puddle of material was gathered around her feet, Mom looking funny and young with a veil pinned up on her head and hanging around her shoulders, Mom wearing bangs,

Mom holding a bouquet of white flowers just like in a bride magazine picture, and there, next to her, Richard's father. Mom must have buried the photo somewhere in the attic, and Richard had found it. I had to swallow twice just to see his face—he looked so handsome and nice—and he looked almost exactly like Richard!

Richard, so much like his real father—the same chin and hair, and the same smile! I stuck the photograph back into the box and was just closing it when I spotted something else in the box I'd missed.

A little key was lying in the corner— a little gold key, the kind that might open an old-fashioned locket—or the shining gold lock on the trunk in our attic!

"What do you think you're doing, you creaky kid?"

Richard's voice boomed from the door; I'd been so absorbed in my thoughts that I didn't hear him come in. I was caught.

"Spy!"

His eyes were wild. I was scared practically to black death, but happy to see him. He'd come back.

I didn't know what to say, but I had the little key in my hand and now curled my fingers tight around it. "Give it to me!" Richard said under his breath. "Right now!"

I didn't answer. I just stood there squeezing the key in my hand.

"Did you hear me?" he whispered. Dad and Mom were on the patio and I could hear their voices drifting up through the open windows.

"You look just like your father, Richard," I said.

"Hand it over," Richard said with murder in his voice.

"No!" I said.

He couldn't try to take it out of my hand; I'd scream the place down and he knew it.

"Give me the key, Carolyn Frankfurter!" he whispered.

"Won't work!" I said.

"I need it!" he said.

"You have to give the stuff back," I said, "or I'll give the key to Dad and he will."

Richard stood there glowering at me. Although he'd never really hit me hard, I thought I was in for it now. He made a fist and raised his arm. Suddenly he shook his head, punched the fist into his other hand, and said a bad word. His eyes looked horrible, as if someone had just kicked him in the stomach. Then a sound came out of his throat and I got really scared. Oh, no, was he going to start to cry again? "I need the key. I'm going to sell the stuff," Richard said.

"You can't. It's not yours."

He flopped down on his bed, practically heaved his back against the wall, and put his knees up against his chest. "I have to have money. I'm going to New Mexico," Richard said.

I knew he'd wanted that all along—to see his real father face to face, wherever he was. I remembered the beat-up old suitcase he'd bought for fifty cents at the Covellis' garage sale, and that was over a year ago.

I just stood there thinking it over. I was still holding the key tight in my fist, not moving. Right above Richard's bed I saw it again—the empty place where the kite had hung. I thought that maybe there was something like that in Richard's life—a big blank where his father should have been.

I guess that's why I opened my hand and gave him the key.

During the night, I couldn't sleep. Maybe it was because of the heat. Or maybe it was that I kept imagining Richard carrying his old, beat-up suitcase, trying to hitch a ride on a superhighway in the middle of the night.

The next day I went to the bank and took out the money I'd been putting into my account all summer. I didn't really need *Death of a Rock Star* or silver earrings. I brought the money to Richard when he was getting dressed to go out after dinner. He was standing in front of the mirror over his dresser, combing his hair.

His eyes got so narrow all I could see were his eyelashes. "Where did you get this money?" he asked. He put down his comb to count the bills, then he looked at me.

"Never mind. Just take it," I said. He'd forgotten Mrs. Covelli had paid me for cat-sitting, but I didn't remind him. I hadn't spent much of what Dad had paid me for chores, but I didn't tell him that either. I could have told him it was the sum total of my summer savings. Why didn't I?

"Where did you get this money?" he asked again. His eyelashes seemed almost stuck together.

"Take it," I said.

After a moment of suspicious silence, his voice dropped so low it came out sounding like a strum on a bass string. "You *stole* it," he said.

I think my mouth flew open.

"You copy everything I do!" he suddenly yelled, and he grabbed the bills and crushed them in his hand. His skin was pulled tight across his knuckles and he was waving his hands. I'd seen him looking wild before, but never like this.

I didn't answer. It was like the time I'd driven to the club with Flim and yelled, "Floor it!" when what I really wanted was for him to slow down. I wanted to tell him it wasn't stolen, but I couldn't. Maybe I wanted him to think I had stolen it—and was going to be just like him, a thief.

"You wouldn't!"

I didn't speak, I didn't move.

"Ohmygod!" Richard said. He leaped past me, flew out

the door of his room, and ran into the bathroom. I followed him, yelling, "Richard!" but it was too late.

He was tearing the bills, my money, my twenty-four dollars of savings, into pieces, throwing them into the toilet. He flushed it, watched the bits of money whirl away, while I stood there, horrified.

Then he spun around to face me. His face was almost the color of the red-flowered wallpaper behind him, and his voice was spooky-strange. I got a chill. "Don't. You. Ever. Steal. Anything. Again!" he said, and the words sounded almost like an echo coming from behind the walls.

That same night, while my parents were out at an open-air concert, Richard and Flim-flam took the stuff out of our attic. The key, the photo, and the cigar box had vanished from his room, and now at last the stuff was going too.

I heard them first in the attic, then in the garage.

If I stand at the basement door and leave it open a crack, I can hear everything and see most of what goes on.

They'd moved Flim-flam's car in there and were loading the trunk. What if the Covellis heard them too, saw the green plastic lawn bags filled like Santa's sack in the back? Hurry, hurry! What was taking so long?

"I don't care. Next week is Labor Day. I'm getting it out of here early," Richard said. "I want it out of here today! A week isn't going to make a big difference."

"Well, it turns out the friend of a friend I thought would buy it won't be back until October—so what am I going to do with it? If we keep it here just a few more weeks—"

"Out of this house," Richard was saying. "Tonight. And forget the money. I don't want it. It's all yours. And look—don't surface here for a while, huh? My father doesn't want me to cut it with you."

Flim-flam let out one of his acid laughs. "Now I'm the heavy, huh, Mother?" he said, and then he spotted me at the door. "Hey, what is *she* doing here?" he yelled.

Richard swiveled on his heels. "Get back upstairs," he ordered, and I left, but not before I'd seen it again—the silver knife with the black handle, bigger than the knife we use to slice bread—and this time it was lying on the front seat of Flim-flam's car.

But even then, I thought it was over. I heard Flim-flam's car leave and knew the stuff was out of our house for good. I went out to the yard and looked up at the last of the summer stars; school would be starting, Jen and Barbara were coming home, Mom and Dad and Richard and I would settle back into family routine. Richard would get a job and earn the money to go to New Mexico, and maybe once he saw his real father, he'd be the old Richard again.

I felt so relaxed I fell asleep right there in the yard lying in the webbed chaise and didn't wake up until my parents returned from the concert at almost eleven o'clock. My mother was smiling down at me. "You must really have been tired," she said. "Long day, Carolyn?"

I was still woozy, so I just yawned.

"Long summer," Dad said, smiling.

"Guess what?" Mom said. She sat next to me on the chaise and lowered her voice as if she was going to tell me a big secret. "We met the Strawheims at the concert tonight, and Mrs. Strawheim's baby is due next week. She told me she thought you were one of the loveliest young ladies at the club. And" —Mom was smiling ear to ear telling me this—"if the baby is a girl, she plans to name it—are you ready for this?—Carolyn!"

No, I was not ready for that. Mrs. Strawheim, about to

name her baby after me while her penlight was still upstairs in Richard's room, her five stolen dollars—where? I looked up at the sky and picked a little star and made myself and that star a promise. I'd return what I could to the Strawheims and even, if possible, to the Covellis. As soon as I could.

EIGHTEEN

"Didn't you promise you were going to paint the locker floor when the summer was over?" Dad asked Richard on the third Saturday in September.

After Labor Day the club closes, the swimming pool is drained, the lifeguards' chairs are put away, and the awnings over the Deck disappear. Everything is deserted and quiet.

"I can't do it today. I've got three leaf-raking jobs this weekend," Richard said to Dad, so I jumped right in. I said I'd paint the locker floor myself, right after morning rehearsals.

Jen and Barbara and I had joined the Junior High Drama Club and were so busy rehearsing for *As You Like It* that I was hardly home anymore.

Things had quieted down at our house, and although Dad and Richard didn't shoot baskets in the yard or sit around watching football games together on TV, at least they weren't fighting. Richard was out most of the time doing whatever odd jobs he could find, and Dad was busy preparing for a trip to Washington to speak to some legislators about dental health insurance.

"You sure you can manage painting it alone?" Dad asked me.

"Very easy," I said. I remembered the promise I'd made to myself to return Mrs. Strawheim's penlight and five dollars. Her baby had been born and I had pasted the announcement ("It's a Girl! Carolyn Patricia, 6 lbs., 6 oz.") in my life scrapbook. I'd taken the penlight out of Richard's room and had it in the back of my closet in a shoebox. If Dad agreed to pay me five dollars in advance, I could slip the penlight and money right under the door of her locker. Mr. Strawheim was sure to sweep out his locker in a week or two and find it.

"It's a deal," Dad said, smiling at me. "How about dark gray?"

"Green," I said.

"Okay, green," he agreed, and he winked. "Like Aunt Agnes's eyes."

I had the stuff in a brown bag: a can of Gossamer Green paint, a paintbrush, newspapers and rags for cleanup, and a paint stirrer the man at the hardware store had given me free. In the back pocket of my jeans I also had the penlight and the five dollars in a white envelope. Dad felt five dollars was a fair price, and he didn't mind paying in advance. I told him I needed it for something important, and because he was very busy preparing his speech, he handed me a five-dollar bill without any questions.

At the club I put my bike in the empty bike rack and now the place really *was* deserted; the locker doors looked bleak and gray and not at all friendly. The sky was overcast, too, with just a bit of sun slanting through clouds here and there.

My feet seemed to creak with every step, and I had the strange feeling that someone I couldn't see was here, watching.

Ridiculous. It was cool, a little damp, the pool was

closed—no one would come to sit on the beach on a day like this. There were some people playing tennis, but the courts were far away, at the other end of the club.

I creaked my way through the row of lockers, reached ours, and set down my bag. First I would go to the Strawheims' locker, slip the pen and money under the door, and then, with that off my mind once and for all, spend the rest of the day painting our floor.

Why did I keep feeling so jumpy? I stood in front of locker 114, reached into my back pocket, and pulled out the white envelope with the flashlight and money. It was sealed with cellophane tape and looked like every other plain white envelope in the United States of America, except that it had my fingerprints all over it.

Stupid. No one was going to brush this envelope with powder to look for invisible fingerprints. I started sort of a mental conversation with myself: *Five dollars and a penlight is no case for the FBI, Carolyn. Relax.*

I got on my knees and pushed the envelope neatly under the Strawheims' locker door. Simple and easy. Stay cool, Carolyn.

All done. I got up, turned, and, in a cold flash of horror, saw Mr. Prisco, the club manager, staring at me from the open door of locker 119. He'd been fixing the door hinge and was still holding a can of oil in his hand. The look on his face when he spotted me was like nothing I'd ever seen. I didn't know a person's eyebrows could travel that far up and still stay on his head.

I immediately thought that I would throw up. I felt as if I had just swallowed four milkshakes and a suitcase of French fries. The planks under my feet were swaying exactly the way our living room floor had swayed when Patrolman Quinn was standing in our front hall.

Now Mr. Prisco's high eyebrows made one neat line across his forehead. His bald head seemed bigger, as if it had grown since summer. "Aren't you one of the Desmond children?" he asked, striding toward me. No "Hello" or "How are you?"—just dark suspicion.

I nodded. The milkshakes I hadn't had churned in my stomach.

"What are you doing here?" he asked.

"I, uh, came to paint the floor of our locker," I managed to say.

He looked at me, at the locker, then back at me. "Is this your locker?" he asked. He was very close to me now. I could see the fillings in his teeth when he spoke.

"Yes. No." What was I saying? "I got the lockers mixed up," I said.

He was watching my eyes, my nose, my mouth. Four of his fingers came up to his face and he rubbed the side of his chin. Then his fingers stopped. He'd spotted the painting stuff I'd left in front of our locker. "What's in the bag, sweetheart?" he asked. He didn't say "sweetheart" in a sweetheart way.

"My painting stuff," I said. *Congratulations, Carolyn, you got it out.* He probably hadn't seen me slip the envelope under Mrs. Strawheim's door or he would have asked me about that first.

"Let's have a look inside the brown bag," he suggested. His voice was so tough I imagined it was two or three hard voices braided together.

We walked down to the locker together. I pulled everything out of the bag to show him. Nothing in the bag but newspapers, rags, the paint, the brush, and the stirrer. He squinted into the empty bag, picked it up, turned it upside down. "Is this your locker?" he asked, looking at our locker door.

"I think it is," I said. Maybe he'd believe a twelve-year-old was dumb enough to forget her locker number three weeks after Labor Day?

No. "Let's see your key," he said.

I reached into the other back pocket of my jeans and took out the key. He took it out of my hand and looked at the number on the key; then he looked at the number on the door. "Why don't you open the locker and let's look inside," he said. It was not a question. It was a command.

What did he expect to find in there—the crown jewels of Europe? My hand shook so much that he finally took the key himself, stuck it into the lock, and creaked it open, one two three.

The locker door swung open and there, bunched in the far corner and looking to me like an overweight dragon, was the green plastic bag, bulging with the stuff Flim-flam and Richard had stolen. There was a tear in the bag and part of a camera was sticking out; I didn't have to see the rest to imagine the tape recorders, radios, cassettes, and the guitar I'd seen under Richard's bed two months ago stuffed inside.

Mr. Prisco's eyes were red-hot balls bulging out from under his way-up eyebrows. *Oh, Richard, how could you mess us up like this?*

"Good lord in heaven!" Mr. Prisco breathed.

After a pause, though, when he spoke again, the razor blades and hatchets had gone right out of his voice. I could hardly hear him. "Okay, let's go, sweetheart," he said. "Come with me."

Then it hit me. Richard hadn't put the stuff there at all! It was Flim-flam who'd carted the stuff away. He must have taken Richard's locker key and unloaded the stolen stuff here, so that Richard would be blamed for everything.

He'd flim-flammed my brother, but good.

NINETEEN

"I think we got the thief," Mr. Prisco said to his secretary, Miss Douglas, the minute we got into his office in the clubhouse. "Sit there, young lady," he said to me, and pointed to a leather chair under a picture of the club's founder, Admiral Roger Van Slyker.

I sat down and took deep breaths, which is what my mother used to tell me to do whenever I felt carsick when I was a little kid.

I took deep breaths while Mr. Prisco called my father, and I took deep breaths while he called the police. I took more deep breaths while Mr. Prisco rubbed his hands together and told Miss Douglas how times were changing. "Miss Douglas, crime, crime, crime. It's all you read in the newspapers these days," and how he'd not spared the rod for his own three boys, who were now respectable grown men out on their own and had never been in trouble in their lives. "And look at this one," he said, pointing to me. "Just a baby. What a pity! What a disappointment for the parents!"

Miss Douglas agreed that times really were changing. She

said she'd never heard of bike locks and burglar alarms and guard dogs until ten years ago.

The policeman came just as she was saying that things were getting completely out of control. It wasn't Patrolman Quinn, but an older policeman with white hair and a pot belly, sort of like a Santa Claus dressed in the wrong costume. Patrolman Butkowski. He must have just eaten lunch, because he had crumbs on his chin. I saw them when he leaned over and asked me how old I was.

I couldn't speak. If they had handed me a pad and pencil I might have written down 12, but no sound could come out of my sick throat right now.

It didn't seem to matter to Patrolman Butkowski whether I answered or not. I guess he was used to silent crooks.

"How do you spell 'Desmond'?" he asked Mr. Prisco. Mr. Prisco spelled our name, looked us up in the club directory, and recited our address and telephone number.

"They been members here for a while?"

"Since I've been here. And I've been here nine years," Mr. Prisco said.

"Unusual for a kid this young..." Patrolman Butkowski said. "Although not unheard of, either."

"Any other kids in the family?"

"I think there's an older boy," Mr. Prisco said, and he suddenly looked uncomfortable, as if someone had stepped on his foot. He'd remembered Richard.

"Maybe we better get him down here, too," Patrolman Butkowski suggested.

Mr. Prisco looked even more uneasy. Remembering Richard, I guessed he realized he could have made a mistake. He looked at me and then he looked at the telephone. "I'll call Dr. Desmond back, ask him to bring the boy," he said.

"Not necessary to call. I brought him, he's here," a voice

said. Dad stepped into the office and, yes, there was Richard right behind him. They must have broken all speed limits to get here so fast. Or maybe it just seemed fast to me. I was in no hurry to see the scene that was coming.

Richard was so sweaty, he looked as if Dad had turned the hose on him. His face was dripping and his shirt was stuck to him, front and back.

The first thing I noticed about Dad was that he'd buttoned his shirt wrong. Then I noticed his hair, which was neatly combed in the front but was sticking out every which way in the back. "I'm Donald Desmond," he said. "And this is my son, Richard."

There was a second of silence. Then the policeman said, "We found a cache of stolen goods in your locker, Dr. Desmond."

"So Mr. Prisco said," my father said.

"Your daughter was found trying to enter yet another locker," Patrolman Butkowski said.

"Is that right, Carolyn?" My father's eyes looked horribly confused.

"No!" I managed. "I wasn't trying to get into another locker. I was just returning—"

"*Returning?*" Patrolman Butkowski asked, when I couldn't finish.

"Returning five dollars," I said.

"That you took?"

"She's got nothing to do with this," Richard suddenly blurted out. His head was bowed and he wasn't looking at me. Or anyone. "She's just a little kid, for crying out loud."

My father's hand came out and touched my shoulder, and I jumped up and said, "I have to go to the bathroom." I should have said, "I have to *run* to the bathroom," I was so sure I was going to be sick. I leaped up and ran out; no one stopped me.

As I flew out of the office, I heard Richard say, "It wasn't her, so leave her alone, will ya? It was me. I took the stuff, all of it."

I didn't throw up after all. I just stood over the toilet for a couple of minutes until the feeling passed. Then I went to the sink and splashed cold water on my face and looked in the mirror and told myself to stay cool and go back in there and tell everyone that sometimes being a thief is like a disease you catch when your resistance is low, that Richard had caught it from Flim-flam, and that now Richard had recovered and was well again. Then I realized that nothing I said would help. Richard had stolen or helped steal the things in the green plastic bag, and no matter whose idea it was, he was just plain guilty.

When I got back to the office, my mother had arrived. Dad had left a note for her on the refrigerator door, and she'd found it the minute she came in from the supermarket. She was sitting on the edge of a chair now, with about a hundred crumpled wet tissues in her hands. She kept putting the tissues into the corner of first one eye and then the other. She looked the way she did once when she had a two-week cold that turned into bronchitis, and she wouldn't look at me or at Richard. Her face looked as if the lower half, her mouth and chin, were ready to crumple, too. I suddenly felt as if I were the mother and she was the twelve-year-old, and I wanted to go over and put my arms around *her*.

I didn't, though; Dad's expression was inky-black rage—I think I'd never been afraid of my own father until this minute. He didn't look like my father at all.

"I'm afraid we have to take Richard to the station," Patrolman Butkowski said, and flipped closed the pad he'd been writing in.

"Before we go," my father said, "I want to ask Richard something."

Richard's face looked like a death mask. I shuddered. Out of the window I could see the beach and the water beyond it. Compared with the upheaval in here, everything outside seemed as flat and calm as a picture painted on the wall.

Dad walked over to an empty chair and put his hands on its back. I looked up at the portrait of Admiral Van Slyker and imagined his eyes were following him and that he could hear everything.

"How could you?" Dad said. "Coming from the sort of home you've had, the sort of family we are, how could you have done what you've been taught all your life is morally wrong?"

I wished I were out of here, walking along the sand, all by myself.

Richard didn't answer, didn't move. If someone had said, "Richard is dead," I wouldn't have been surprised.

My father's voice broke. "When did you learn to steal? Son, how could you have turned from my wonderful small boy into a . . . a *sneak thief*?"

Richard's head moved. Just a very tiny bit to the left, toward Dad. "I'm not your son," he said. His shirt, his face, and now his eyes were shiny wet. *"Don't you remember?"*

My mother cried, "Richard!" into the tissue at her mouth.

Dad closed his eyes and shook his head. "No, I don't. I keep forgetting. Why can't you?"

"Because I can't be Doctor Wonderful! I'm just me, Richard, son of Mr. Nobody!"

My father lifted the chair off the floor, and now I really did think it was going to come flying across the room. There was no telling, with that new face, what he was going to do.

Outside, on the flat water, little sailboats with white sails drifted in every direction.

Mr. Prisco looked nervous. He took a step forward and said, "Dr. Desmond," and his fierce face didn't look fierce at all any more. He looked like an ordinary, nervous bald man, like someone's grandfather.

My father didn't throw the chair. He lifted it a bit and then slammed it back down on the floor. It sounded like a rifle shot.

"So you think stealing is going to make you Mr. Big?" Dad cried. Richard didn't answer.

"Did you hear the question?" Dad asked. His voice went volcanic. His hurricane tempers were nothing compared with this.

No answer from Richard.

My mother's white face grew whiter. "Don——"

"Answer me, Richard, damn you!"

Richard shook his head and started to cry. Not big sobs, this time, just little silent tears he tried to cover by turning his head and putting his arm across his eyes. Worse, much worse than sobs.

My eyes kept going to the window and the boats. I remembered sitting in Cookie's sunfish, skimming through the water on that first hot summer afternoon. It seemed a hundred years ago.

"Maybe we ought to just go to the station," Patrolman Butkowski said. I was terrified. Not handcuffs, please. Not Richard in handcuffs.

"Wait a minute!" my father shouted. We just all stood there, too startled to move. Dad bounded across to Richard's chair and grabbed Richard by the front of his soaked shirt. He pulled him up to his feet, lifted his arm, and slapped him hard across the cheek. It was the first time I'd ever seen Dad hit

Richard. Richard's head jerked forward, a thunderstruck look on his face.

Then, having completely stunned us, Dad recoiled. His voice hurtled from a shout to a whisper. "It's because I still love you, Richard, I honest-to-God love you," he said, squeezing shut his eyes, and he threw his arms around Richard and held him tight. "I'm sorry," he said. Then he kissed my brother where his cheek was still bright pink from the slap.

It was the first time I'd ever seen Dad kiss Richard.

It was the first time I'd ever seen tears in my father's eyes.

TWENTY

We followed the police car to the station. No lights flashing, no chains or handcuffs, no sirens, no nothing. Richard sat in the front seat with Dad, and Mom and I sat together in the back. Mom was resting her head against the side window, and the only thing she said during the whole trip was that the car air-conditioner was turned up too high. She shivered a couple of times.

I'd never been in a police station. This one looked like a private house on the outside, something like Jen's house, only with an American flag on the front lawn. Inside, what might have once been a living room or dining room or kitchen was now offices with hard floors and large desks—and more flags. Policemen were everywhere, but it turned out that Richard would not be booked or fingerprinted by any of them the way I'd imagined from watching television crime shows. Instead, I sat on a bench alone in the hall while Mom and Dad and Richard went into the youth officer's office on the second floor.

I had to sit and wait a very long time, which gave me time to think. I didn't know exactly what they would do to my brother, but my eyes found a star on an American flag hanging over the stairs, and I made a wish: *Don't send my brother away. Give him another chance.* He'd messed himself up this summer, but there had been so many other summers before this one, and winters and springs, too, when he was a lot more good kid than bad kid, a kind of normal mixture you'd find in anybody, sort of like my life scrapbook, filled with good stuff and bad stuff. The things people were ashamed of they'd keep quiet, but it was certain that everybody, including all the policemen in this room, including Mr. Prisco, the Covellis, and even Mrs. Strawheim, had at least one under-wraps, hush-hush secret.

A few minutes later, the youth officer, who was not dressed in a uniform and looked more like a gym teacher than a policeman, followed Richard, Dad, and Mom down the stairs and said the hearing would be in six weeks but not to worry. "First offenders under sixteen are generally treated leniently by the judge," he said, and he even smiled under his moustache and said that we looked like a pretty supportive family, and he shook everyone's hand, including mine. Richard looked relieved, but he was still damp and his eyes looked as if he hadn't slept since last week.

"Supportive" is what the youth officer had called us and that's what I wanted to be. I didn't know how to tell Richard that although I hated him sometimes, I loved him in heavier doses than I hated him. "Do you want a piece of gum?" I asked him, remembering I had some in the side pocket of my jeans. It was all I could think of to say.

"No, thanks," Richard said. "I don't want gum. I'm just thirsty."

That's when my father really floored me. "I'm thirsty, too," he said, and he added, "Let's stop for a soda on the way home."

My father, offering to stop for a *soda*? I couldn't believe my ears. Even my mother looked as if she hadn't heard right. "A *soda*, Don?"

"Just for once, I suppose it won't kill us."

Later, when we were sitting in the car with our paper cups filled with Coke, Mom said, "No one can live by the rules all the time," and I think she was talking mainly to Richard.

Dad quickly added, "But we're not going to make a habit of this." I noticed that he'd already taken a big sip of his soda and was diving in again. "I must admit it is pretty refreshing," he mumbled over the cup.

Then he got more serious and he said, "I think it's time to tell you I'm not very perfect at all." He moved the cup away from his mouth and turned to Richard. He hesitated, as if what he was about to say was something he'd been holding back for maybe years. "I nearly flunked out of college when I was a junior. I guess I never mentioned that I was not the best student."

I had to stop my mouth from opening in amazement. I couldn't picture Dad a poor student, or a poor anything.

Dad continued, "I ought to add a few other things I guess I should have told you a long time ago. I've misread a few x-rays in my life, called something a cavity when it was only a shadow, although I suppose that's an error any dentist could make. But once, I pulled the wrong molar, and that's a secret I'd rather you didn't share with anyone.

"Another thing, it's not the instructions that are wrong when I try to put stuff like picnic tables together. It's not the tools or the glue or the screws or the nails, either. It's me. I've never been able to assemble anything right in my life."

Richard wasn't answering, but he was listening.

"I've never been able to work out my income tax form. I never could get it right without a lot of help. And I'll tell you something else. I was the only kid in my town who flunked his driver's test four times. I'm not kidding."

Mom was rolling the ice cubes around in her paper cup. "You forgot something else, Don," she said.

"What's that?" Dad asked. He'd finished his soda and was wiping his mouth with a napkin.

"You can't spell. You can't spell to save your life."

There it was when we got home, pinned by a magnet to the refrigerator door, the note Dad had left for Mom when he was called by Mr. Prisco: TROUBLE AT THE CLUB. COME OVER IMMEDIATLEY. In big black marker letters, where no one could miss it, he'd spelled "immediately" wrong.

Richard looked at the note and, believe it or not, he smiled. The funny thing is he must have read a million other things Dad had misspelled but never noticed the mistakes before.

Dad looked really embarrassed. "Of course, I was in a hurry," he said, and Mom gave him a who-are-we-kidding look.

"Do you mind if I keep the note?" Richard asked Dad.

"Are you serious? What for?" Dad wanted to know.

"I've got a big blank space on the wall over my bed and I want to fill it," Richard said, and he took the note off the refrigerator door. I knew what he meant. He wanted a reminder that Dad was not someone faultless, a big trophy winner, the sort of shining example he'd never be able to match, but an ordinary human after all.

"You can keep it, but don't hang it," Dad said. He put his arm around Richard's shoulder and he added, "I've got a better idea. It's my turn to buy you a kite. This time you can help me put it together. If we work as a team, we'll get it to fly, don't you think?"

Richard never stole anything after that, and when he and Dad and Mom and our family's lawyer went to the hearing, I got my star wish. The judge dismissed the charge and Richard's case was closed. All the stolen stuff including the money went back to the owners, and my mother told me the judge called Richard a "successful salvage."

Still, everything did not turn out to be exactly all right again. Cookie returned the whistle and creamer to Richard, and Richard brought them over to Mrs. Covelli and apologized, but things had changed. Cookie never spoke to Richard again, and although Mrs. Covelli was still always nice to me, she never asked me to take care of Aunt Agnes after that. As for Flim-flam, he was held responsible for his part in all the thefts, was discovered to be carrying the marijuana mixed with oregano, and worst of all, was caught pulling a knife on the ticket seller at the New Madison train station. I was sure it was the knife I'd seen in his car, and for weeks and weeks I kept having terrible dreams about it. Finally, Flim-flam was "remanded to Stone Bridges," a minimum-security prison in North Williamston and was never seen at our house again.

I didn't miss Flim-flam much, but I did miss the club. Dad and Mom had to resign after the news about Richard got around. In a way, I was glad I wouldn't have to face Mrs. Strawheim or all our old friends, and although Dad said we would join the Field and Golf Club in East Loomis, it won't be the same. I sometimes think of our bright yellow locker and wonder who'll be using it next year.

In a way, nothing will be the same. Once, when I was walking in the school corridor, I heard some kid say, "Did you hear about her brother?" but I kept walking very fast and never even saw who the kid was. Then, on the school bus, a bunch of kids from our neighborhood started a big whispering chain about me that lasted for ten blocks, and when I got off at my stop they all yelled, "Who'd your father pay to keep Stickyfingers out of jail?"

And last week, Richard came in wearing a really neat seadiver's watch and I saw Dad's eyebrows go up. "Where'd you get that?" he asked right away, and Richard explained he was just holding it for a guy who found it got in his way during basketball practice and that he'd forgotten to return it. He said he'd return it tomorrow. Dad nodded and seemed to believe Richard, but there was a minute of uncomfortable silence as if Richard were waiting for another question, as if he thought Dad had to be absolutely sure.

And I can't be positive that if I ever see something shining under Richard's bed I won't go flying in to see if it might, just possibly, be something that doesn't belong to him.

On the program of *As You Like It*, my name appeared as "Carolyn F. Desmond." Between the first act and the second, while we were sitting there in our costumes and makeup, Jen and Barbara asked me what the "F" stood for. I felt I'd kept my secret long enough. "Frankfurter," I said, loud and clear.

They nearly died laughing. "I don't believe in secrets, not anymore," I said. Now that it was out, it felt good, as if I'd freed myself of a dark bat I'd been keeping locked in a cage.

"I've got to tell you something," Barbara said. "Remember when Mr. Gold, the music teacher, got a love letter, unsigned, in his mailbox?"

"Yes!" Jen and I both said.

"I wrote it," Barb admitted.

"No kidding!"

We started to giggle again.

"I had such a thing for him," Barbara said.

Then Jen got very quiet. "I think Jen has a secret, too," Barbara said, and Jen nodded.

"I have," she said. "I haven't told anyone."

"Try us. It'll feel good."

Jen took a deep breath. "While I was out in Utah, visiting my grandma, my father was on TV. On a talk show, late at night."

"Wow! Why would you want to keep that a secret?"

"'Cause he talked about his facelift. He told the whole world how he had all his wrinkles ironed out."

We all nearly collapsed laughing.

Letting out those secrets felt really great. Believe it or not.